NEW YORK REVIEW BOOKS
CLASSICS

# THE JOKERS

ALBERT COSSERY (1913–2008) was a Cairo-born French writer
of Lebanese and Greek Orthodox Syrian descent who settled in Paris
at the end of the Second World War and lived there for the rest of
his life. The son of an illiterate mother and a newspaper-reading
father with a private income from inherited property, Cossery was
educated from a young age in French schools, where he received his
baccalauréat and developed a love of classical literature. At age
seventeen he made a trip to the French capital with the intention of
continuing his studies there. Instead he joined the Egyptian
merchant marine, eventually serving as chief steward on the Port
Said–New York line. When he was twenty-seven his first book,
*Men God Forgot*, was published in Cairo and, with the help of
Henry Miller, in the United States. In 1945 he returned to Paris to
write and live alongside some of the most influential writers and
artists of the last century, including Albert Camus, Jean-Paul
Sartre, Tristan Tzara, Alberto Giacometti, Lawrence Durrell, and
Jean Genet. He was also, briefly, married to the actress Monique
Chaumette. In 1990 Cossery was awarded the Grand Prix de la
francophonie de l'Académie française and in 2005 the Grand Prix
Poncetton de la Société des gens de lettres. His books, which have
been translated into more than fifteen languages, include *The House
of Certain Death*, *The Lazy Ones*, and *Proud Beggars*.

ANNA MOSCHOVAKIS has translated *The Engagement* by
Georges Simenon and *The Possession* by Annie Ernaux.

JAMES BUCHAN's latest novel is *The Gate of Air*.

# THE JOKERS

ALBERT COSSERY

*Translated from the French by*
ANNA MOSCHOVAKIS

*Introduction by*
JAMES BUCHAN

NEW YORK REVIEW BOOKS

*New York*

THIS IS A NEW YORK REVIEW BOOK
PUBLISHED BY THE NEW YORK REVIEW OF BOOKS
435 Hudson Street, New York, NY 10014
www.nyrb.com

First published in France by Joëlle Losfeld, 1993

*Cet ouvrage publié dans le cadre du programme d'aide à la publication bénéficie du soutien du Ministère des Affaires Etrangères et du Service Culturel de l'Ambassade de France représenté aux Etats-Unis*

This work, published as part of a program of aid for publication, received support from the French Ministry of Foreign Affairs and the Cultural Service of the French Embassy in the United States.

Library of Congress Cataloging-in-Publication Data
Cossery, Albert, 1913–2008.
[Violence et la dérision. English]
The jokers / by Albert Cossery ; translated [from the French] by Anna Moschovakis ; introduction by James Buchan.
  p. cm. — (New York Review Books classics)
ISBN 978-1-59017-325-1 (alk. paper)
1. Government, Resistance to— Middle East— Fiction. 2. Satire. 3. Humorous fiction. I. Moschovakis, Anna. II. Title.
PQ2605.O725V513 2010
843'.912— dc22

2010013738

ISBN 978-1-59017-325-1

Printed in the United States of America on acid-free paper.
10 9 8 7 6 5 4 3 2 1

# INTRODUCTION

ALBERT Cossery is a novelist all on his own. As consistent in his themes as in his sedentary habits, he published every ten years or so of a long life a novel written in French and set (with a single exception) in Egypt.

Since his death in Paris in 2008, Cossery's blend of low-life nostalgia and philosophical dandyism has won new readers in France and, in rather lesser numbers, in Egypt and Lebanon. This sparkling novel, first published as *La violence et la dérision* by Julliard in Paris in 1964, is the sixth of his nine books to be translated into English.

Cossery was born in 1913 in Cairo into a Greek Orthodox family with some private means. Educated in the French schools of Cairo, Cossery was drawn to both surrealism and Baudelaire and, at the age of eighteen, published a book of verse, *Les morsures* (Bites), which I have not been able to locate.

After a cruise as a ship's steward to the United States, where he seems to have met Henry Miller, he published in Cairo in 1941 a book of five surrealist stories, *Les hommes oubliés de Dieu*, translated as *Men God Forgot* and praised by Miller. The book found its way to Algiers where it came to the attention of both Edmond Charlot, publisher of Albert Camus, and Camus himself. Cossery's first novel, *La maison de la mort certaine* (translated as *The House of Certain Death*), came out in Cairo in 1944. With the liberation of Paris, Cossery moved there as did Charlot, who republished both books.

At some point, Cossery married. The marriage was a failure, though whether this was a cause or an effect of Cossery's contempt for women, or both, I cannot tell. At the end of 1945, he installed himself in the hotel La Louisiane in the Latin Quarter, where he was to live (first in Room 58 and then in Room 70) for the next sixty years. Like his characters, Cossery rose late. He frequented literary cafés such as the Café de Flore and the Deux Magots and devoted himself to affairs of gallantry. His pose of extreme indolence concealed, as with Stevenson, a heroic industry.

*The House of Certain Death*, in which indigent tenants await the imminent and inevitable collapse of their slum house, sets out Cossery's principal themes. Like Baudelaire, he has neither compassion nor sympathy for the poor, only a limitless curiosity. Cossery is fascinated by the division of labor in the very pit of society. His monkey men, melon sellers, sweepers, repairers of kerosene stoves, cigarette-stub pickers are echoes of Baudelaire's *chiffonniers* (rag pickers). Cossery is entranced by very, very small sums of government money: the one-millième piece (about a quarter of a U.S. cent) that the women of the house pay for a guide to the address of the slum's landlord, the two-piastre piece (a nickel) that buys a night in a hotel with only three eiderdowns for twenty guests.

Laid over the Arabic notion of *'eish* (the easy life) is a sort of Cynicism, derived either from his own reading of Greek literature or by way of Camus. Like Diogenes of Sinope, the original Cynic or "dog philosopher," who lived in his own filth and told Alexander the Great to get out of his light, Cossery's heroes do not seek virtue, knowledge, or salvation, but, in a world that is raving mad, only a natural and malodorous contentment. Cossery's manifesto is: The most terrible thing is not to be poor, but to be ashamed of it.

There followed, in 1948, again with Charlot, the most beautiful of all his books and his farewell to surrealism, *Les fainéants dans la vallée fertile*, translated as *The Lazy Ones*. Here a family of men, engulfed in an antedeluvian lethargy, or *paresse séculaire*, in a filthy villa in the Nile delta, continually besieged, ambushed, and overwhelmed by sleep, confront a crisis when their father considers taking a wife. There are passages of such otherworldly comedy you might be reading the first chapters of the *Quixote*.

Cossery's next novel was his longest and least satisfactory, *Mendiants et orgueilleux* (1955), translated as *Proud Beggars*. Here a university professor sinks into hashish and serene penury. For no reason at all, he murders a sixteen-year-old prostitute.

Having walked straight into the capital paradox of the Cynic's philosophy, Cossery then withdrew from his exposed philosophical positions. Beginning with *The Jokers*, the characters diminish in number and become more dandified. The scene is swept a little and given a lick of paint. The insurrectionary spirit that flickers at the end of *The House of Certain Death* gives way to a more subtle protest.

Against bourgeois society, with its tyrannies, pitiable privileges, and futile exertions, Cossery pits *flânerie*, idleness, nonchalance, ridicule, and the insolence and sexual frigidity of the dandy. In *The Jokers*, which is set in Alexandria, the local governor has declared war on beggars and idlers. There are distant echoes of the revolutionary debates of the age, from the Situationists to Fanon, but those are submerged in comedy. *Un complot de saltimbanques* (1975), translated as *A Splendid Conspiracy*, and *Une ambition dans le désert* (1984), which is set in the only Persian Gulf sheikhdom without any petroleum, are variations of this theme.

In Cossery's final novel, *Les couleurs de l'infamie*, published in 1999 but portraying Cairo in a sort of perpetual early 1970s, the slumlord who is the moral villain of *The House of Certain Death* is now a bent real-estate developer whose building has just collapsed, killing all its tenants. "We are not," he tells the dandies with a profound self-satisfaction, "in the age of the Pharaohs. One must build for a limited period or that would be the end of the developer."

Meanwhile, the professions of the poor have lost their demarcations. They are now "unemployed workers, craftsmen without customers, intellectuals that have lost hope in fame, petty officials turned out of their offices for lack of chairs, university graduates bent double under the weight of their sterile learning, and finally those given to eternal laughter, the philosophers, who, loving shade and peace and quiet, consider the spectacular deterioration of the city to have been especially brought about to sharpen their critical senses." The hero is a pickpocket. The philosopher-dandy of Cossery's final novel lives not, like old Diogenes, in a broken pot but in what is nearly as good: a tomb in Cairo's City of the Dead.

As the French are the wittiest race in Europe, so are the Egyptians in Africa. Cossery's comedy derives from the contraposition of exquisite French and an exceptionally squalid setting. His is not the French I learned at school, let alone that spoken nowadays in metropolitan France, but he writes sentences of which Balzac would have been proud. His style depends for its effect on precise and outlandish adjectives, as in the description here of the terrace of the Globe Café. That is not the very best style in English, which likes verbs and nouns, and presents a challenge to his translator.

Cossery has his faults. There is a certain rigidity of posture, which is open to parody, and, most notably in *Proud Beggars*, a daft nihilism. There is not the slightest inquiry as to why the poor of Egypt are poor nor, in a country that passed in Cossery's lifetime from British protectorate, to parliamentary monarchy, then to military junta, nationalist autocracy, and dynastic republic, any sense of history or process in the affairs of humanity. To nobody's surprise but Cossery's, the Arab world has chosen not derision but violence.

Cossery has a superstitious terror of family life and makes no attempt to penetrate it. Females shed all interest at puberty, or, as with Soad in this novel, at the moment they put up their hair. Thenceforth, Cossery's women are *commères, acariâtres, mégères*—gossips, old bags, shrews.

Cossery writes in French not just because he needs the urbanity and distance of a foreign language to display his Cairo and Alexandria but because God writes in Arabic, which brings all kinds of entanglements. Cossery's achievement, substantial as it is, lacks the audacity and toughness of the Egyptian novelists in Arabic such as Naguib Mahfouz, Yahya Haqqi, or Taha Husain. Yet Mahfouz has many more readers in French and English translation than in his native Arabic, so perhaps Cossery has the last laugh.

—JAMES BUCHAN

# THE JOKERS

# I

THE DAY promised to be exceptionally torrid. The policeman, who had just taken up his position at the city's most distinguished intersection, suddenly felt that he had fallen prey to a mirage. It had to be the sweat pouring down his gloomy features, making him resemble a designated mourner in the midst of a funeral service, that was interfering with his vision; he blinked several times, as if to remedy his defective eyesight and get a sharper perspective on things, but this feeble effort was to no avail. So he pulled a red-and-white-checkered handkerchief—as coarse and dirty as a dishrag—from his pocket and mopped his face vigorously. Having thus clarified his view of the world (at least for a moment), he turned his gaze on the mirage—and received a shock. For what he saw—insofar as he could make out anything distinctly—was a beggar, a finer specimen than he'd seen in a long time, lounging comfortably at the corner of a brand-new, quite splendid building, one that contained a bank and a jeweler, no less: two aspects, in other words, of a universal metaphysical order that demanded immediate protection from the rabble. As if driven by murderous rage, the policeman shoved the handkerchief back into his pocket and, blinking continually so as not to lose the benefit of his newfound sight, lunged straight at the impudent wretch. Orders had gone out a month ago: the city must be liberated from the lowlifes that had taken to swarming like ants at a picnic in even the most respectable streets. This was one of many directives that the new governor—a man bursting with bold initiatives—had issued, and admittedly, it was the most difficult to carry out. The new governor's ambition was to clean up the streets and protect them from any further blots upon their honor; he talked about streets as if they were people. So, after the prostitutes, the street vendors, the cigarette-butt collectors, and other minor scofflaws, he had set his sights on the beggars, a peaceful race with such deep roots in the soil that no presumptive conqueror before him had ever succeeded in exterminating it. It was as if he wanted to disburden the desert of its sand.

So the policeman, this zealous servant of a mighty state, threw himself at the beggar (whose very serenity was a kind of provocation), roundly berating him according to rules of a time-tested art. But the beggar failed to react to these insults, murderous though they were. He was an old man, hideously wrinkled, with a gray beard that swallowed up the whole of his face and a head that vanished under an enormous turban. His eyes were closed, and the thick black circles under them gave him an epicene appearance altogether unusual for a bum. What's more, he was dressed in a fanciful multi-colored outfit better suited to a street acrobat than to a man in his condition. This eccentric old man, the ancestor of his eternally persecuted race, seemed sunk in a deep sleep that even the deafening roar of the countless cars fighting through the intersection could not disturb. At last, realizing the futility of his insults and orders, the cop gave the bum a kick, and then another kick, to knock him out of his infuriating inertia. He was just about to kick him again when he saw the beggar abandon his initial position and slump to the ground, where he assumed the proud and thoroughly disdainful attitude of the dead. For a moment, the policeman thought he'd killed him and was seized with panic at the thought of having lost his prey. A dead beggar was worth less than nothing; it might even get him fired. He needed this bum to be alive. Bending over the old man, he grabbed him by his turban, shaking him with savage fury in an attempt to bring him back to life. This action was both rash and irreparable: as if by magic, the beggar's head became detached from his neck and remained stuck to the turban, which the policeman continued to brandish in the air like a bloody trophy. The crowd of gawkers that had gathered around the two protagonists let out a collective cry of horror and spewed an indignant stream of outrage at the policeman, who, dropping his trophy, stared at the baying pack of dogs with the look of someone suffering from stomach cramps. It took awhile before the high spirits that had been excited by the morning carnage succumbed to the realization that it was all a hoax. What had at first appeared to be a genuine flesh-and-blood beggar was in fact only a dummy, ably made up by a skilled artist, that had been left out in this respectable neighborhood precisely in order to provoke the police. Far from calming the crowd, this discovery incited it to an opposite extreme; people began to snigger and sneer at the unfortunate cop, who stood there stunned. Faced with this jeering mob, their jibes piercing his uniform like so many darts, the poor man took up his regulation whistle and let out a series of shrill blasts in the hopes of attracting some of his more courageous colleagues from nearby patrols. But his summons went unheard, and in any case the crowd was already dispersing, having had its fun for the day. People returned to their private difficulties and disappointments, each recounting the story in his own fashion, but always with the sense of gleeful malice that is felt on the street whenever some representative of authority is dealt a blow.

## 2

A KILOMETER away, in a room located on the roof terrace of a six-story building by the sea, young Karim, the instigator of this farce, was hardly gloating over his attack on the governor's authority. He wasn't even thinking about it. Lying on his bed, shirtless, his fingers busily twisting a lock of hair on his forehead, he looked as lazy as a bored monarch, glutted with wealth and pleasure. Karim gave himself up to a feeling of delicious languor, while enjoying the voluptuous vision of his mistress from the night before getting dressed in the middle of the room. From the patronizing smile that played on his lips you would have thought he was observing a procession of dancers, lasciviously swaying their hips for his pleasure alone, instead of a poor creature (picked up on the street) whose modest charms no longer held a single secret for him. Karim's languorous pose was meant to suggest an atmosphere of luxury and decadence, but in fact it hid the state of nervous tension that had been racking him since he woke up. As always on such occasions, Karim had produced the effect with an end in mind: it set the scene for a special stratagem he had developed to discourage the venality of his fleeting lovers. The success of the stratagem was certain, and yet every time he deployed it his heart beat wildly. Now the moment when he would be forced to show his cards was inexorably approaching.

Young Karim was no novice; he'd had ample experience, and there was almost no chance of the business going wrong. The little prostitute, whom he'd brought home after planting the bogus beggar at the intersection, certainly wasn't about to make a scene; she wasn't the type. At worst, she might get angry—but Karim didn't care about that, since he had no intention of seeing her ever again. In fact, the disappointment with which her pathetic comedy was almost certain to end didn't concern him in the least; the denouement would be what it was. He just wanted to get rid of her as quickly as possible. The slowness and care with which she was getting dressed was beginning to exasperate him. He was in a hurry; he couldn't wait for her to be gone and leave him alone at last. The girl no longer amused him. Other, more interesting things—they happen all the time—must be occurring on the surface of the earth, and to appreciate them properly he had to be either by himself or in the company of friends who would be able to understand. Inconceivable to share such delicate pleasures with a woman! Women were completely impervious to his kind of worldly humor; they could never fully appreciate the inherent absurdity, for example, of a government minister's speech, while they took seriously the buffoonery of the tyrants in power. No doubt this one was just as dim as all the others; aside from the sweet nothings that enliven love play, Karim had nothing to say to her.

While she dressed, he continued to gaze at her with that patronizing smile of a bored monarch, as if conferring a favor upon her. The girl was putting on her shoes, her face bowed, her neck humble. Karim was annoyed by her silence. He detected a reproach. Did she suspect something? At last she slipped into her dress and was done.

The moment of truth had arrived. With the nobility of a great and generous man who hates to bring up the topic of money, Karim said:

"Zouzou, my dear! Before you leave, reach into my jacket pocket and take what you want."

The girl stood motionless, visibly disconcerted by this invitation; for a moment her eyes scanned the room—in search of the jacket, perhaps—but then she lowered her gaze, as if suddenly overcome by shame. She was a very young girl, with the face of a child and a touchingly sweet look. From her humble manner you could easily tell that she was new to her profession. Her cotton-print dress, modest bearing, and discreet makeup made her look more like a schoolgirl than a courtesan. Her story was sad. On the previous evening, she'd been fleeing the governor's henchmen when Karim accosted her, then invited her—according to his usual princely custom—to spend the night in his apartment (a grandiose word that Karim would have used for an empty lot if it were so privileged as to claim him for a resident). The girl had allowed herself to be seduced; what other choice did she have?

She remained silent, irresolute—a heartbreaking sight! A few steps away Karim's jacket hung from the back of a chair; unfortunately, its pockets were empty, or almost. Any money she'd find there wouldn't feed a bird, not even if it was starving. Karim eyed the girl, his uncertainty growing by the second. What was she going to do? Go over to the chair and rifle through the pockets of his jacket? The little slut! Would she dare to take him at his word? Hadn't he treated her like a princess? Wasn't she satisfied by the passion he'd displayed during their endless night of love? Karim recalled his heated declarations; hadn't he gone so far as to propose marriage? Honestly, he'd neglected nothing in his efforts to seduce her. Would she tarnish his reputation and, with one petty gesture, ruin a love affair that had begun so well? How stupid!

The silence was unbearable. Karim was about to open his mouth to try to rescue the situation, when at last the girl spoke:

"Oh! No thanks. This has been just fine."

The bet was won; now Karim could insist without risk. Stretching his arms and letting his head fall on the pillow, he yawned splendidly.

"Oh yes, I insist. Go on, take what you want. Otherwise I'll be mad."

"Another time," said the girl. "I don't need anything just now."

The refusal appeared to disturb Karim; he waxed sentimental.

"Zouzou, you're hurting my feelings. I thought we were more than strangers. Everything I have is yours. Don't you love me anymore?"

"I didn't mean to cause offense," the girl said—she seemed to realize the wrong she'd done to the young man. "It's impossible for me to take your money. You've been so kind."

"And all because I love you—that's why," Karim responded; the girl's words had made him quite sure of the efficacy of his method. "But I won't make you take anything. Do as you please. This is your home now, too; we're like man and wife."

She smiled sadly, perhaps at the enormity of the lie, perhaps because she sensed the impossibility of ever being his wife. Without a word, she grabbed her handbag from the table and prepared to leave. Only then did Karim realize just how young she was, and how devastating her forlorn look and timid smile could be.

They'd had their long night of love, but this was the first time he'd really looked at her—not through the veil of desire but as a human being, hunted and defenseless. What he saw was so painful that he forgot about the whole decadent-monarch act; the dancers with lascivious hips disappeared; all that remained in the room was a depressing, and very real, spectacle. There was no doubt: the girl had brought tragedy with her. Karim hadn't expected such a cruel twist of fate; now what had taken place seemed monstrous. How pathetic, he thought, to see myself falling prey to remorse! He tried not to succumb to such weakness, but the pity went straight to his gut. He was overcome with a need to do something for the girl. To help her in some way, not let her leave like this. How? Propping himself up on his elbow, he looked hopefully at his jacket, as if he might discover a hidden treasure in its pockets; in his confusion, he was counting on a miracle. He thought about what apart from money he might offer her, at least as a token of goodwill. Finally, he had it! It was so simple: he'd ask her name. Zouzou was what Karim called all his conquests—not only because it was convenient but also so as not to retain any precise memories of them. With this girl it would be different. He almost wept to think of her leaving him without telling him her name. All of a sudden, that knowledge took on a mysterious importance.

With infinite sweetness, he inquired:

"What's your name?"

She hesitated before responding. Clearly this sudden sign of interest touched her.

"My name's Amar," she said.

"Well, Amar, I'm delighted to have met you. Come see me often. I'm counting on you."

"May I, really?" she said with a glimmer of happiness in her eyes. "I wouldn't be disturbing you?"

"Not at all. On the contrary. This is your home. Didn't I say that?"

"That makes me very happy. I'll go now."

He thought he should get up, walk over, and kiss her, but then he was reluctant to prolong things further. The girl broke his heart; anything more, and he might get depressed. He stayed put.

"So long then," he said, still lying down.

Before she left, she thanked him with rare civility for the night she'd spent under his roof. To hear her you would have thought she'd been showered with kindness and respect. Perplexed, Karim imagined that she'd guessed his game and that her friendly words were steeped in vicious mockery. But that wasn't likely; this girl exuded candor and honesty. Karim was ashamed of having taken advantage of her innocence; once again, he felt overcome by regret. In the end, it was she who had the upper hand. He realized that now.

Amar opened the door onto the sun-drenched terrace, and the light entered the room.

"Leave it open," Karim said.

Hearing the outer door close behind the girl, Karim felt relieved of a heavy weight. Finally he could breathe freely! He jumped out of bed, tied the drawstring of his pajamas, and went out onto the terrace. For the week or so in which he'd occupied this room, where he enjoyed a superb view of the sea (a nice change from his previous place, so dark and airless, a real hovel in a rough neighborhood), he'd woken up each morning in good spirits. Every day the first thing he did was to go out on the terrace and revel in the spectacle afforded by his privileged position. He still hadn't gotten over the novelty of it: even reading the paper, until now the most essential ingredient of his happiness (proving as it did that the universe was fertile with insanity of all kinds), now came second to this daily tour of the horizon. Like an explorer looking down from the top of a mountain, Karim gazed from his sixth floor onto the city, its multiple haunts filled with cretins and crooks going about their business. The thought of a whole society given over to sheer bloody-minded rapacity gave him limitless pleasure. More and more, he thought of his new residence as an observatory, in which his sense of humor could be nurtured and blossom freely.

He leaned on the brick parapet that surrounded the terrace and stared out at the sea. It extended brilliantly, like a mirror, all the way to the far-off point where the horizon was veiled in haze. The city stretched out to the left and right, with its gleaming modern buildings projecting a false image of a flourishing city. Almost no one would suspect the immensity of the slums, filled with disgusting hovels and ancient filth, that lay hidden behind the façade. Karim felt the heat of the sun on his bare chest; he took a deep breath, then leaned over to look at the paved road that ran beneath the cliff, continuing along the shore for several kilometers. It was a wide two-lane avenue with a sidewalk where in the evening pedestrians came to breathe the sea air and snack on watermelon seeds. Cars sped by furiously, looking from a distance like malfunctioning mechanical toys. Sometimes, to Karim's delight, the driver of a horse cart dozing in his seat added a human note to the infernal race toward annihilation. But it was increasingly rare to see anyone taking a break. The police were cracking down on the lazy and the carefree, judging such attitudes to be crimes against the nation. An entire civilization, an entire way of life, easygoing and debonair, was about to disappear. On the sidewalk, there were only a few people, all walking by at a rapid pace, racing to God knows where. Something in the landscape had changed: not the least sign of a bum sleeping in the sun; not a single body sprawled out or squatting on the street. Begging had been driven underground. And where had the beggars gone? It was unlikely they were all working in factories. Where, then?

It was such a pity! The absence of beggars on the cliff road was a sign of changing times. This idiot governor, with his absurd ideas, had succeeded in fundamentally altering the city. Karim wondered what had become of the dummy he'd dumped off in the middle of the European Quarter last night. Had they discovered him yet? He wished he'd been there when the police had apprehended the bogus beggar; he'd missed out on a good laugh. Maybe there'd be something about it in the papers. But there was no counting on it. The papers were all in the governor's pay; they'd never dare to publish a story that might turn him into a laughingstock for kids. So what? The governor himself would hear about this farcical attack on his orders. His thick skull would shatter to pieces—he'd never expect them to come after him in such an unusual fashion. Up to now, he'd been happy to arrest the odd member of the underground revolutionary party, an easy target over the years for whatever governor happened to be in power. Having thus made a show of strength, and having resolved, in the manner of his glorious predecessors, the problem of opposition in the laboring classes, the governor believed his interests to be safe from any damaging propaganda. He was familiar with only one kind of subversive spirit: those scattered individuals who, intransigent in their hatred, sought glory through action and were willing to lay down their lives for the sake of the right and the good. Men who took themselves seriously, in other words, like him. How could he have suspected that the city was also home to a new, budding breed of revolutionary, scathing and funny, for whom he and his kind all over the world were nothing but puppets pulled by strings, their words and gestures nothing but the grotesque convulsions of a buffoon. Karim could see that terrible things lay in store for the governor. He'd find himself overwhelmed by a new kind of insurrection and wouldn't know how to react. There'd been entertainment value in the bogus beggar, but that was only a trifle compared to the immense, crazy plot that was now under way. Karim knew that his friend and accomplice, the incomparable Heykal, was currently working on a secret plan of such subtlety and scope that it would destroy the governor's authority for good. To tell the truth, Karim wasn't sure just what was being plotted;

Heykal had been mysterious about the details of his jolly conspiracy. But now Karim had proof that the launch of the secret offensive was imminent: Heykal had finally decided to meet with Khaled Omar, the businessman, and he had asked Karim to take a message to Omar arranging a meeting that very night. That this meeting was taking place showed that Heykal had developed a plan of attack and that he required material assistance in its execution; Khaled Omar's fortune and generosity of spirit could be invaluable to the cause. Tonight, then, would bring news: at last, Heykal would unveil his plans. The meeting was to take place in a café in the European Quarter, and Heykal had requested to speak to the businessman alone; clearly, he wanted to ply his charms in private. Karim wasn't worried about how things would turn out. Heykal exerted an irresistible influence over everyone he met; Khaled Omar would certainly be convinced. There really was no resisting Heykal.

It was still too early to visit the businessman; he didn't get to his office before late morning. Killing time, Karim wandered around the terrace, dreaming of all the trials he and his friends had cooked up for the wretched governor. And yet, the memory of the young prostitute he'd tricked with his declarations of undying love continued to trouble him. He swore that if he saw her again, he'd offer her money or a present of some kind. Soothed by this altruistic thought, he went back inside and headed straight to the corner where there was a pile of kites of all sizes and colors, some still unfinished. For several months, Karim's favorite activity had been making kites, which he sold to a candy seller who had a shop nearby and a loyal clientele of children. In an era of propeller planes, young Karim found it wildly appealing to resist the nefarious progress of a world infatuated with the mechanical by making kites—such superbly frivolous toys. He felt a reassuring sense of joy whenever he saw them in the sky—lightweight, peaceful constructions taunting the ponderous planes, those crude machines devoid of poetry.

He rummaged briefly through the pile of kites and finished by digging up one that was still in a skeletal state, but whose frame, made from reeds that he'd trimmed down and cinched together with string, suggested a kite of astonishing size. He grabbed a pair of scissors, some rolls of colored paper, and a dish, in which he mixed flour and water to form a paste. Returning to the terrace with this assortment of materials, he laid the frame of the kite on the flagstone floor, crouched down, and set to work with the focus and intensity of an expert building a rocket to the moon.

Lost in his work, Karim took no notice of the pathetic character who'd come onto the terrace and now stood near the door to the stairwell, trying in vain to catch his breath. This pale, miserable individual, some fifty years of age, carried a folder under his arm and in his hand a closed umbrella, on which he leaned, trembling. He continued to gasp for a moment, then suffered a coughing fit which, returning repeatedly, nearly choked him. At the first sound of the violent cough Karim lifted his head and stared, dumbfounded, at the intruder. The man returned his gaze like someone meeting an acquaintance in a crowd without much pleasure.

"Are you Karim?"

"Yes, that's me. What's this about?"

"Police," said the man. "I've been ordered to conduct an investigation with regard to you."

Without taking his eyes off the man Karim jumped to his feet. Funny kind of cop! In this heat he was dressed to endure the rigors of a harsh winter, in a dark, heavy suit with a wool scarf around his neck. His thin face bore a wary, concerned look but not a severe one—the sort of gravity commonly found on the faces of people condemned to an early death. And he was on the brink of exhaustion. For a man of his age, the six flights he'd just climbed must have constituted a dangerous feat. Out on the terrace in the blinding sun, he couldn't see clearly; he opened his umbrella and, in its welcome shade, began to scrutinize the young man. This comical pose restored Karim's confidence; his worries fell away. He walked up to the policeman.

"So what's the subject of this investigation?"

"Couldn't we go inside? I'd like to sit down. I need to speak to you."

"It would be an honor!" Karim said. "Come in!"

The policeman closed his umbrella and entered the room. Unfazed, Karim followed. He wondered, though, what the reason for the investigation could be. It had been a long time since he'd tangled with the authorities. That they could have identified him—so quickly!—as the man behind the bogus beggar was inconceivable. Unless they were psychic! Hardly likely. Well, it would soon become clear. The face of this timid, asthmatic policeman seemed like a good omen to him.

Karim never forgot his manners.

"Please, Your Excellency, have a seat! I do hope you'll forgive the mess. I've just moved in."

"Not a problem. This isn't a social visit."

The policeman sat, gasping as before, but more weakly now. Karim discreetly reached for his jacket and put it on, covering his bare chest; he'd just remembered that it was important to be properly attired in front of a representative of the law—even one who was suffocating to death from asthma. Since he'd known Heykal—that is, since he'd come to appreciate the comic side of life, with its many ridiculous passions—Karim had renounced all dignity in his dealings with people who possessed even a modicum of power. Better to play the fool, to act dumb as a post; it was the only way to throw them off. Heykal had explained to him that dignity existed only between equals who shared a mutual respect. Maintaining your dignity before a police officer, or any other agent of the powers that be, meant absolutely nothing. Faced with a mad dog, the only intelligent thing to do is run. As to those individuals who, in the immensity of the world, deserved to be treated with dignity, they were few and far between. The risk of running into one of them was negligible.

Karim buttoned his jacket and sat down. Then, as if expecting a message of the utmost importance, he said:

"I'm listening."

The strange policeman opened his folder. He pulled out a piece of paper and consulted it.

"Have you lived here long?"

"About a week. As you can see, I'm still settling in. I'm going to completely renovate the place. I'd lined up a carpenter, but unfortunately he just lost his wife, and I've been left hanging. I need to find another one."

The policeman sighed and shook his head, as if it was painful for him to destroy such a beautiful plan.

"You'd do better to hold off," he said.

"Why?"

"Because you can't live here. It won't be permitted."

"What do you mean 'permitted'?"

The officer's eyes narrowed to a point, and he leaned toward Karim as if to reveal a terrible secret.

"Did you know, my friend, that this building lies on a strategic route!"

This declaration could only provoke hilarity, but Karim remained imperturbable. Not the slightest smile crossed his face. On the contrary, he appeared to be deeply impressed by what he'd just heard. In a tone of contrition—the tone of a citizen thoroughly invested in the well-being of the state—he replied:

"The cliff road, a strategic route! I had no idea, Your Excellency! On my honor, I didn't know."

"Well, I am informing you now. You should know that the cliff road is a strategic route of the utmost importance. Politicians, heads of foreign states, and prestigious military officials often take this road."

"That's true," said Karim, "but I don't see what that has to do with me."

"You really don't see?"

"No, by Allah I don't! I'm trying to understand, but I don't."

"Well, I'll have to tell you then. It's like this: You are a dangerous man."

"Me? What do they have against me?"

"Nothing, at the moment," the policeman admitted. "But you're on our black list. We've had dealings with you in the past, right?"

"That's true, I won't deny it. But it was years ago, under the previous government."

Again the policeman shook his head, gazing with pity at Karim: such arguments were beyond stupid. Really, these revolutionaries were disarmingly naive.

"If you didn't like the previous government," he said, "there's no reason why you should like this one. We know all about hotheads like you."

Karim was dumbstruck by the brilliant accuracy of this analysis. What could he say? And yet he wasn't going to be thrown off track by the whims of one lousy cop. He had to go all the way to the end.

He protested his good faith.

"How wrong you are, Your Excellency! Me, dislike the government? You'd have to be blind not to love it. Look at me: Am I blind? I'll tell you in all frankness that I look up to the current government the way I look up to my own father. What more can I say to show my respect?"

"Since you brought it up, where is your father?"

"He's dead," Karim replied. "I'm an orphan."

Either out of gratitude—the scene was a gift from heaven—or because he wanted to play his role of repentant rebel to the hilt, Karim was soon on the verge of tears. With his head in his hands, he began mumbling—almost sobbing—about his bad luck, about the unhappiness he'd endured since childhood. He did everything he could to make the whole melodrama seem real, and though he may not have been entirely convincing, the policeman appeared to relent a little at last, remaining silent as he waited for the painful moment to pass. But Karim kept going, talking about his poor mother, dead from a mysterious disease (strongly resembling asthma), the symptoms and effects of which he described with the precision of a trained physician.

Hearing this, the policeman's eyes grew a little sad. His features took on a defeated, depressed look. He'd been in his job for thirty years; there was nothing left for him to learn about the vicissitudes of existence. His skepticism about the benefits of the rule of law, as well as his total lack of ambition, had kept him in the lower ranks of a profession in which cynicism and brutality were the only virtues that counted. A deep human sympathy made him feel a kinship with his fellow man. This young man could have been his son; he was touched by his suffering, whether fake or real.

"How do you get by? Do you work?"

"Of course," said Karim. "I'm in manufacturing."

"Manufacturing of what?"

"I manufacture kites."

"You're pulling my leg."

"I wouldn't dare, Your Excellency! It's the truth. There's nothing extraordinary about it. You've just never thought of it. Look, I'll show you some samples of my work."

He got up quickly and walked over to the corner where the kites were stored. He chose two of different shape and color, and holding one in each hand he lifted them up so the policeman could admire them at leisure.

"Look. You see these kites; I made them. There are no others like them, not even abroad. I have orders from every corner of the world. Soon I'm going to have to take on some help."

The policeman, who still didn't want to believe this story, stared at the two kites like objects in a dream. As much as he wanted to write a positive report, he knew he could never demonstrate that the manufacture of kites constituted honest work. And yet, he thought, these kites—someone made them; they didn't grow on trees. But how could he tell his superiors that a former revolutionary, a subversive spirit, had devoted himself to such a pursuit, without drawing any suspicion to himself?

"It's not serious," he said. "If I put this in my report, I'll be the one accused of making fun of the authorities."

"But why? There's nothing bad about it. It's a modest living, of course, but it gives joy to thousands of children who play with kites. How can you hold it against me, Your Excellency, that I'm interested in making children happy? Today's children are tomorrow's heroes, right? I understand that to a casual observer these kites seem like a childish pastime. But when you think about it, you begin to understand that in practicing this peaceful sport, the children acquire a robust constitution and a healthy view of society, which helps to turn them into good, law-abiding citizens. In other words, as you can't help but see, I labor in the national interest."

The policeman listened to this long outburst with growing discomfort; this young man surprised him more and more. If he wasn't a revolutionary, he had to be, at the very least, quite mad. The policeman thought about his report; he foresaw problems.

"If I may," broke in Karim after a silence.

"Please."

"Do you have children?"

Now he was asking personal questions. What next? Was his wife pretty?

"Yes, I have children. May God preserve them."

"How old are they?"

"The oldest is thirteen."

"What a marvelous coincidence! Would you permit me to offer them one of these kites? It would be an honor as well as a pleasure."

The policeman resisted, but politely, not making a fuss.

"If I'm not mistaken, this is an attempt to bribe an officer of the law. I will be obliged to mention it in my report."

"To bribe you!" exclaimed Karim. "May the sky fall on my head! Your Excellency, you've hurt my feelings. Believe me, I love children. So much so that whenever I see one, tears spring to my eyes. I don't understand how you could misconstrue my offer as an attempted bribe. It was an impulsive gesture; my intentions were noble and pure. I'll be insulted if you reject my humble offering."

And, once again, his eyes filled with tears!

This was a terrible test of the will. The whole investigation was disconcerting—it was so out of the ordinary. Could the young man be in earnest? The policeman thought it was possible. Those proud, stubborn revolutionaries would never talk like this, let alone break down and cry. That was evidence enough that he wasn't mistaken. But strangely this certitude—he didn't know why—made him sad.

What would happen to the world if all the revolutionaries repented and reformed? It seemed to him that a light, somewhere, would go out.

Karim had put one of the kites back on the pile; he held the other out to the policeman, in a beseeching gesture. His face wore an expression of intolerable moral suffering.

"You can't do this to me!"

The officer's compassionate character made him vulnerable. He felt vaguely guilty of impoliteness. The most basic civility demanded that he not refuse a gift offered with such fervor.

Perhaps it was the very meagerness of the gift that finally convinced him to accept. He coughed to clear his voice.

"Well, then, thank you. But I'll take the smallest one."

"I am your servant," Karim blurted out. "You do me unspeakable honor."

Taking the policeman by the arm, he invited him to choose. The policeman, after a moment of hesitation, chose the smallest kite he could find; he hadn't forgotten the issue of transport. He saw himself lugging the cumbersome toy home, unable to hide his burden.

"With my compliments," said Karim. "I hope that the children enjoy it."

"For their sake, thank you," the policeman said, as he turned toward the door. "I must write my report. You'll receive a summons shortly."

"Your visit has comforted me enormously," Karim replied. "I felt alone and abandoned. Believe me, I'm so grateful."

He escorted the policeman onto the terrace and to the door of the stairway, bowing continually. For several minutes he continued to maintain an attitude of artificial deference, then, all at once, he burst into laughter.

He couldn't stop laughing. The cliff road had become a strategic route! Ah! The sick bastards! They had strategic routes now! What presumption! They'd make use of anything to enhance their prestige. But to make him move for so stupid a reason! That was the limit! It was of the utmost importance that he respond to this threat. He wouldn't let himself be evicted; he wouldn't give them the pleasure. First of all, he had to do something about this miserable policeman before he had a chance to write his report. Karim felt sure he'd brought him around, but you never knew. He'd ended up taking a kite; why wouldn't he take more? Karim decided to turn the whole business over to Khaled Omar, the businessman. Khaled Omar, thanks to his contacts at every level of society, would be able to get to the policeman—or his superiors! Khaled Omar could afford to bribe an army of bureaucrats. Karim collected his materials and brought them back into the room. He dressed hastily. It was time to go visit his rich friend.

Outside the house, he paused briefly, contemplating the strategic route with a malicious glint in his eye. He felt a strong desire to piss on it.

# 3

KHALED Omar, an illiterate man, had made his professional debut where some businessmen finish their careers: in prison. A few short years ago he had been a penniless drifter—perpetually hungry, sleeping on the streets, living off thievery and handouts. But Providence, for mysterious reasons, had planned a glorious future for him. Caught red-handed picking a wallet from someone's pocket, he was arrested and given a sentence of eighteen months. This unhappy circumstance was the prelude to his ascent into prosperity, for it was behind prison bars that he discovered his vocation and his star began to rise. Freed from the dread of starvation, no longer worried about his survival, his frustrated but now awakening spirit began to notice a host of things he'd never had the chance to appreciate. Looking around him, he was fascinated by the prevailing economic phenomena of a society condemned to isolation. The black market inside the prison made a powerful impression on him. At first he couldn't participate; he had nothing to sell and nothing with which to buy anything. So he bought on credit and sold his new acquisitions at a profit. The simplicity of this operation astounded him. For the first time in his life he'd made money without expending the slightest effort. In no time, he became a shrewd speculator. He had an innate sense of the laws of supply and demand, and by the end of six months he controlled every transaction and regulated prices at will. He provided the prisoners with supplies of all kinds: cigarettes, drugs, sometimes even women. The jailers, practical men, supported his enterprise; he made it worth their while. By the end, he'd turned prison smuggling into a veritable branch of the national economy.

When he was released, in possession of some cash—and, more important, of a flair for business—he hurried to put on a suit and good shoes and to don a tarboosh. Then, having rented himself an office, he embarked on a number of legal and quasi-legal operations, always with success. He now owned several buildings, along with beautiful land in the most fertile regions, and he continued to conduct his affairs while exerting himself as little as possible. He limited his activities to talking on the telephone with people he never saw. Despite his prosperity, despite his fancy exterior and elegant airs, he retained his peasant manners and his common speech. He only liked vagabonds and only enjoyed the company of unemployed eccentrics whose time was their own. His easy rise to riches had opened his eyes to the fraudulence of the world: he understood that such a thing could not be possible except among madmen and thieves.

His office was made in the image of his rugged spirit. Situated in a back alley of the port, it was striking for its complete lack of paperwork, account books, and the other nonsense businesses employ to create confusion with an imposing appearance. All you could see was a table dominated by an old-fashioned telephone, two wicker armchairs, and a few wooden crates stacked in a corner against the wall, covered in dust.

When Karim showed up just before noon, Khaled Omar was in the middle of a phone call. He waved to his visitor with his free hand, to indicate that his conversation was nearing an end. Karim sat down in one of the wicker chairs and admired the businessman's technique. Slouched in his swivel chair, Khaled Omar listened to his interlocutor, punctuating the conversation with a nod of the head or a curt word. From time to time he let out a sigh, as if to make it clear that he was sacrificing precious time. There wasn't a scrap of paper or a pencil on the table. He kept everything in his head.

Khaled Omar put down the receiver and swiveled to face Karim; thunderous laughter burst out as if from the depths of his being. It was the laugh of an ecstatic animal, irrational and physical to the core.

"So, my young friend! How's your health? Do you know what that fellow on the phone was asking me?"

"No," said Karim.

"Well, he wanted me to get him a tiger!"

"A tiger? Probably wants to sic it on his mother-in-law. That's pretty funny!"

"Not at all. He's dead serious."

"You don't mean to tell me you have a tiger to sell him?"

"Why not? I'll find him one."

Khaled Omar grabbed the fat amber pipe of a hookah that was on the floor by his feet and lifted it to his lips; he wore rings on every finger. He took a few puffs, exhaling a cloud of dense smoke through his nostrils before continuing:

"You see, my young friend, there was a time when I was always scavenging for a crust of bread and never finding anything, and I started to think bread had never existed except in my imagination, that bakers themselves were mythical creatures. And look at me now: I know where to find a tiger. I know who to call to bring me a tiger, on a leash or in a cage. Isn't that extraordinary?"

He burst into laughter again.

"It's hard to believe!" exclaimed Karim.

"It's very simple," Omar said. "You have to penetrate the right circle. Everything a man desires exists, in fantastic quantities, in a well-guarded stockpile somewhere. Have you ever seen a ton of rice? Neither have I. And yet I've sold millions of tons of it. That's the beauty of business. You don't see it; everything happens behind the scenes. I might as well be selling the wind—that's what's so entertaining."

"You're a sensational man, brother Khaled—let me kiss your cheeks! To think I might never have met you..."

Khaled Omar looked at his visitor with visible pleasure. The friendship that united him with the younger man dated back to his time in prison. Karim was only twenty; he'd been arrested as a "dangerous political element" and incarcerated alongside ordinary criminals. Their first few encounters were fairly painful. When the future businessman heard from Karim's own mouth that he was in jail for political reasons, he laughed in his face: he couldn't help but take him for a pathetic fool. Khaled Omar, a simple, primitive man, couldn't comprehend someone risking his freedom for a motive as essentially abstract as a political cause. In his view, that was pure stupidity. He had nothing to regret about his own imprisonment; yes, he had risked his freedom, but for a tangible end—in this case, a wallet stuffed with cash. Plus he found Karim's whole image ridiculous: these political activists who played the martyr made him sick. But despite all that, he developed a brotherly feeling for the young idealist and helped him out in jail.

"Can I offer you something? A coffee, maybe?"

"Yes," said Karim. "I'd love a coffee."

Khaled Omar stood up, walked around the desk, and went to open the window. A loud murmur rose from the alley, where there was a daily market. The sound of the vendors proclaiming the succulence of their goods broke into the room, rattling it like an earthquake. The businessman yelled down to a coffee vendor across the alley, cutting through the din with his thunderous voice:

"Two coffees! Hey, Achour!"

"Two coffees!" the vendor's voice echoed back.

Khaled Omar quickly closed the window and returned to his seat behind the desk. He seemed amused, as if he'd just remembered a funny story.

"Congratulations on your bogus beggar. What a riot, this morning, when the police found him."

"Tell me, are they talking about it around town?"

"First, the news went around that a cop had slit some old beggar's throat. People were outraged. But in the end, they found out it was a hoax. The police are still at a loss, though. They're trying to hush up the incident in the papers—they think it's a stunt organized by beggars to protest the governor's orders."

"Let them think what they want. We're not done laughing yet. Listen, I came here to tell you that I've set up a meeting with Heykal. Tonight, around eight o'clock, on the terrace of the Globe Café. He wanted me to tell you that he's looking forward to it very much."

"You know that I've wanted this meeting for a long time," Khaled Omar said, a barely perceptible tremor in his voice. "Everything you've told me about him fills me with fellow feeling—I love him like a brother already. He should know he can count on me for anything he wants to undertake; my humble fortune is at his disposal."

"I've told him all that. He feels close to you, too—he already knows you better than I do. He's often spoken of you as a man dear to his heart. And all that without ever having met you. He's sure you won't disappoint him."

"What's he planning? Has he told you anything?"

"No," Karim admitted. "I assume he wants to speak with you first. He needs your help. I'm sure tonight he'll bring you up to date with his projects."

"Are you going to keep sending in your letters to the editor? That was a piece of diabolical genius! I'm still staggered!"

Of late the newspapers' sycophantic treatment of the governor had exceeded every precedent in the history of baseness and servility. If you believed the press, the whole city was singing the odious man's praises; his initiatives and his commitment to their success were the sole topics of conversation. Even his militaristic side was singled out for praise, as if the city were a battleground on which the governor, a former general, was staging a victorious war. This was the situation that Heykal had resolved to exploit. His plan consisted of joining the most staunch celebrants and acolytes in their folly, one-upping them with even more outrageous flattery. So he had his people write letters that were so laudatory of the governor's actions that none of the papers could possibly refuse to publish them: they were sure they were serving the glory of their master.

"Not anymore," said Karim. "Someone high up has forbidden the papers to publish our missives. The last ones we sent were never printed. We seem to have overstepped some limit. You remember the one I wrote myself, comparing the governor to Alexander the Great?"

"I remember it well. You read it to me. It was an outstanding letter!"

"Well, in a certain milieu that letter is still considered a masterpiece of its kind. The paper that published it saw its circulation go up by several hundred in one day. Believe me, it'll go down in posterity as the essence of shameless servility. Government lackeys will mine it for inspiration."

"That's what makes me wish I could read," said Khaled Omar. "Then I could enjoy it whenever I want."

There was a knock on the office door and a young boy, dirty and disheveled and with a club foot, carried a tray with two coffees into the room.

"Here's your coffee, Omar bey!"

"Set them there," said the businessman.

The boy emptied his tray, glanced furtively at the two men, and limped away.

"Actually," said Karim, picking up his cup of coffee, "a horrible thing has happened to me."

"What is it? You're worrying me!"

"Well, not that terrible. Though it's enough to make you split your sides laughing...!"

He told Khaled Omar about the asthmatic policeman's visit—how the cliff road had been promoted to a "strategic route."

Khaled Omar's laugh boomed out again.

"The scoundrels!" he said, once he'd recovered. "Unbelievable! I'm speechless! Or did you just make it up?"

"You flatter me! If only! I admit it took some serious effort not to burst into laughter when he said it. He was clearly a good man, the kind of cop who's too much of a human being to succeed in that job. He must have been stagnating for years; he's not young anymore and none too brilliant. I tried to corrupt him."

"How so?"

"I asked if he had any children. When he said yes, I offered him a kite. He'd only accept a very small one. He chose it himself, then left, telling me that I'd receive a summons shortly."

"Blessed be the day I met you," Omar laughed. "So what can I do to get you out of this little mess?"

"Well, I think if you could reach out to him and make him accept a few kilos of sugar, he'd file a report in my favor."

"I'll drown him in sugar, if that'll help. Anything else?"

"No, nothing. Thank you."

"I'm the one who's thankful. You are gratifying my soul by introducing me to your friend Heykal. No matter what, I'll be in your debt forever."

Khaled Omar had never been in love, but thinking about his meeting with Heykal he felt as impatient as a lover before an assignation. From their talk he anticipated a kind of secret, profound joy, more intoxicating than the most potent carnal pleasure. A man who had the imagination to combat violence and stupidity by praising an executioner to the sky must be something else! Khaled Omar had dreamed of this man for a long time.

# 4

DRAPED in a purple dressing gown, Heykal rose from the divan and, for the tenth time at least, walked to the window. He was at his wit's end, but his expression remained impassive and his gait regal, as if specially learned for visiting royalty in their palaces. The chilly, unflinching glance he cast upon the street conveyed his resignation; for some time already, he'd given up hope of seeing his servant, Siri, appear. He might come back tomorrow or in a week—nobody could say, least of all Heykal. Early in the afternoon, Heykal had sent Siri with his only presentable suit to the neighborhood clothes-presser, and now, at six in the evening, he still hadn't returned. The servant's disappearance left Heykal in a terrible state; he felt like he'd been confined to his apartment with no possibility of leaving. All his other clothes were threadbare, more or less, and for Heykal to wear anything inelegant was out of the question. Such a demanding aesthetic would seem puerile if it hadn't been the manifestation of his essential character. While young Karim liked to put on the airs of a lord with the whores he picked up on the street, Heykal *was* a lord—not by virtue of social rank but because he was endowed with a truly aristocratic nature. His striking manner of dressing, walking, and speaking wasn't the result of rigorous training; he had been born to it.

He moved away from the window, not letting his face betray any bitterness—head high, as if to defy destiny. Siri wouldn't return anytime soon; he'd disappeared into the void, and Heykal's suit with him. This formal suit, already several years old, and which at the moment Heykal could only imagine was being dragged through the filth, was an object of constant concern. What maniacal ruses he'd deployed to keep it safe! Much of his leisure time was consumed by careful efforts to protect it from the slightest speck of dust.

It was an extraordinary suit, made from imported cloth in a discreet dark hue and cut with consummate art by the most capable tailor in the country. Despite the fact that Heykal wore it almost exclusively, it had held its shape well, and with age it had even acquired a certain beauty. It had cost him a pretty penny; but it had been well worth the price, for it fulfilled its role to perfection. When added to his own natural presence, the opulent suit gave Heykal undeniable cachet; he passed, even in the city's wealthiest circles, for a young man of high rank. Though he wasn't rich, he was also not without resources; a meager income from a small inherited plot of land was enough to let him live modestly. Nobody knew the amount of this income, and given his manners and the confidence he projected, he was usually taken to be a wealthy landowner. At thirty-two, he had yet to work; much better to make do on his meager rent than to get involved, even sporadically, with the league of bloodthirsty crooks who populated the planet. But Heykal was no idler; he was perpetually at work, uncovering the absurdity of human behavior. The world of fools pleased him. He would, in fact, have been unhappy to discover that something he'd seen or heard contained even a hint of sense. Sometimes, reading a vaguely sensible piece of news in the paper, he grew sick with annoyance. He delighted in the endless spectacle of man's folly and, like a child at the circus, never failed to find life wildly entertaining.

He glanced at the alarm clock on the chest of drawers. Seven already! The extra time he'd allowed to his servant was over; now he had no choice but to assume the worst. And yet even in private, Heykal didn't let his rage come out in the open; he remained calm and serene, while the sarcastic smile that continually played on his lips turned just slightly ferocious. He lit a cigarette, lay down on the couch, got up again to return to the window. Nothing. He was beginning to get used to the routine. He imagined Siri crushed beneath a tram and felt a kind of peace in the face of the inevitable. His servant's disappearance not only prevented him from leaving but would prevent his rendezvous with Khaled Omar—a man to whom he'd soon be subtly, inexorably linked. It would be deeply upsetting for him to miss this first meeting with the businessman. Ever since Karim told him about Omar—by relating the circumstances of their friendship—Heykal had wanted to meet him. And yet, he'd put it off again and again, wanting to make sure of certain facts about the businessman's character before he did. Perhaps he's also foreseen that one day he might need Omar's help and was waiting for the propitious moment to make his acquaintance. In any case, he'd come to the conclusion that Khaled Omar would, without a doubt, be a valuable associate in a certain spectacle of mockery he had conceived and was preparing to set in motion. According to what Karim had told him, the businessman was hostile to all forms of political conspiracy. He hated politicians and considered them lower than dogs—not living dogs but stinking, dead dogs. Heykal's conspiracy couldn't help but seduce him, given that its goal wasn't to stage a coup or throw a bomb at the governor's head.

This governor was a face—possibly the most ridiculous face—of the universal reign of fraud. Heykal knew him by sight, having often seen him at the municipal casino, surrounded by his most fervent supporters. They formed a sinister crowd of lackeys hovering around him and smiling earnestly at the stupidities he reeled off in an oracular tone. Heykal was so captivated by the man's brute ignorance that he developed a true passion for him: here was someone so tragically stupid that you could only respect him for it. Magnificently and single-handedly he represented the inanity that ruled the world. Heykal was sometimes alarmed by the near-sadistic fascination he felt for him, a man who seemed to have been made governor entirely for Heykal's own personal satisfaction. Each day brought more proof that in his initiatives and public speeches the governor dreamed of nothing so much as making Heykal happy by gratifying his sense of the absurd—as if he suspected that someone, some-where in the city, was just waiting to rejoice over yet another non-sensical deed. As a buffoon he lacked for nothing; how could Heykal not love him? To kill him would be blasphemy. That's what the pigheaded revolutionaries who fought him outright didn't get: that they were giving him a reason to take himself seriously. To Heykal, the crimes of power were so obvious there was no need to shout them in the streets. Even a child could see.

He walked toward the window again but stopped, hearing a faint noise from the corridor. Instantly his anger toward his servant disappeared; he'd been rescued. A few seconds passed before Siri appeared with the famous suit, suspended from a hanger, at the end of his outstretched arm.

"This is what I get for counting on you?"


Siri, the servant, looked at his master with a weary, fatalistic expres-sion on his sleepy face. He never used drugs, but he resembled an addict permanently in need of a fix. With his half-closed eyes, he seemed to be sleeping standing up. This unbreakable bond with sleep that he'd maintained from birth predisposed him to be calm and gave him a generous spirit. Without opening his eyes, he said in a peaceful voice:

"Prince, it's not my fault. Things—"

"What things, dammit! I have an important meeting. I might miss it because of you."

"Sorry, prince," said Siri, cracking a lifeless eye. "But things—"

"Shut up or I'll strangle you," said Heykal. "Now put the suit on the couch."

Siri didn't respond but weakly bowed his head, as if to commu-nicate the unfairness of his reception. With infinite care and sopo-rific slowness, he deposited the precious burden on the couch; then he went to squat in a corner, waiting patiently for his master to deign to speak. But Heykal had stopped paying attention. He was getting dressed in front of the mirrored armoire, pleased at the last-

minute reprieve. It was always like this; he just couldn't stay angry
at his servant for long. Beneath his moronic exterior, Siri possessed
undeniable gifts. Heykal entrusted all material matters to him and
could even go several weeks without giving him money; Siri continued to run the household as if money didn't even exist. There would
always be something to eat at mealtime. How he managed to make
do was a mystery. Heykal suspected Siri of stealing food and staples
from the neighborhood merchants, and one day he figured Siri
would wind up in prison. Then, from time to time, Siri would adopt
the tone of a sage and speak of money as of a necessity that could on
occasion be of some value; he made it sound like a philosophical
discovery—perhaps banal but not without its importance. This discreet allusion to financial difficulties never fell on deaf ears. Heykal
understood by it that his servant had run out of resources. He
would offer a bit of money, and Siri would pretend to refuse, pro-
testing that there was no hurry, that he was not yet on the verge of
ruin. Heykal would insist to the point of becoming angry, and finally, and always reluctantly, Siri would accept the sum.

Seeing that his master had turned his back and was continuing
to get dressed without calling for his services, Siri, head still bowed,
started to mumble under his breath, as if defending himself against
accusations lodged by imaginary characters who placed his loyalty
in doubt. Heykal allowed him a moment to air his grievances before
finally losing patience.

"What now?"

"Prince! It's not fair!"

"What's not fair? Isn't it enough you've made me late for my
meeting? Now I'm expected to listen to your lamentations?"

"Yes, prince, it's not fair. I can't bear for you to be mad at me. I'm
late, it's true, but it's not my fault. I had to save the honor of our
house!"

"The honor of our house! What on earth—Can't you leave me in
peace? Go sleep in the kitchen."

"I don't want to sleep. I have tell you the whole story first."

Still buttoning his shirt, Heykal turned to look at his servant.

He knew all about Siri's stories—shaggy-dog tales, usually slow and hard to follow. But if you had the patience to listen, you'd be rewarded in the end—the ends were fabulous. At another time, Heykal would have listened with pleasure, but right now he was in a hurry to see Khaled Omar. He refused temptation.

"I don't want to hear it," he said.

"I beg you, listen to me. In the name of Allah! I had no other choice. Would you have wanted us to lose face in front of strangers?"

"I don't understand a thing you're saying. Why were we going to lose face?"

Now that he'd aroused his master's curiosity, Siri struck his best raconteur's pose. Squatting comfortably, he cleared his throat and gazed upon his captive audience with a mysterious, world-weary expression.

"Well, prince," he began, "as you know, the shop that belongs to Safi, the clothes-presser, is a popular haunt for the neighborhood notables. They sit there all day philosophizing, smoking, and sipping tea. You'll be happy to know that they hold me in high esteem. These are people of stellar reputation, and they are aware that I serve in your house."

Siri fell quiet and completely closed his eyes, as if the source of his inspiration had suddenly run dry.

"And?" asked Heykal.

"Prince," Siri resumed, "this afternoon, I realized that the situation is serious."

"What situation, mongrel!"

"Listen, prince! How could I let them think that we had only one suit? Every time, they see that it's the same one. They were starting to look at me with pity and to shake their heads suspiciously when I mentioned our splendid dwelling. Don't you understand, our reputation was beginning to slip! So to address the situation I invented a story."

"Go on." Heykal spoke with icy rage. "Right now I have to assume you're on something."

"God save me, no! Don't be angry, prince! I wanted to dispel any doubts about our fortune, so I told them you were especially fond of this suit—despite having an armoire full of clothes—because it reminds you of a love affair that broke your heart. I told them this was the suit you were wearing when you first encountered the wonderful woman who was the greatest love of your life. But, alas! this woman being dead and your happiness gone, you maintain a special fondness for this suit, in her memory. That's all, prince! Is there anything that's not to your honor and credit?"

"And it took you all that time to tell them these idiocies?"

"They wouldn't let me go, prince! They wanted to know all the details of your love affair. For example: What was the name of the lady, how did she die, and were you married? I had to answer every question. I only got away by promising to tell them even more next time."

Looking lazier than ever, Siri rose, retrieved the clothes brush, and went to stand next to Heykal. Everything was settled, he thought. He awaited his master's congratulations.

"So, prince, you're not mad anymore?" he asked.

"It's all right," said Heykal. "I forgive you, though it's the stupidest story I've heard in my life. From now on, leave the honor of the house alone. You nearly made me miss a very important meeting."

"How could I leave the honor of our house alone!" responded Siri, opening not just one eye but both at the same time. It was a sign of powerful emotion. "I'll never let anyone insult you, prince!"

"Give me a handkerchief," Heykal snapped, realizing that the discussion could drag on forever. Honor was his servant's favorite subject.

From the dresser Siri removed an immaculate white handkerchief and presented it to his master, who grabbed it, checking carefully to see that it was spotless, then slipped it into the outer pocket of his jacket. He was now dressed. He inspected himself in the mirror one last time, and, finding himself impeccable in every way, prepared to leave.

This abrupt departure was not to Siri's liking. He would have preferred to talk longer with his master, to share some deep thoughts drawn from his sleepy brain. But sensing that there would be no indulgence this time—Heykal refused to talk—he accepted his cruel fate. Full of foreboding, he asked:

"Your orders, prince?"

"I don't need a thing," Heykal responded. "I'm dining out. Go to bed."

And he disappeared into the corridor, leaving Siri speechless.

# 5

THE LAMPLIGHTER, performing his nightly chore, leaped from one streetlamp to the next like an aerialist, illuminating the twilit evening with a rich, magical glow. His gestures were sweeping and graceful, and Heykal stopped to watch him before venturing into the street. Before he could take two steps, he was hailed by a man who'd been hiding behind a tree. Surprised, Heykal approached the stranger. He stared blankly for a moment before recognizing him. It was an old acquaintance—a man who'd been Heykal's personal beggar for years, who used to wait in front of his door every day. Heykal hadn't seen him since the governor's citywide crackdown on begging.

The man was trembling; his eyes were haggard and bleary; his rags seemed filthier than usual. He whispered hoarsely:

"May Allah help the believers!"

"Yes," said Heykal, "sad times. Where've you been for so long?"

"I was in hiding," responded the man, still in a whisper. "What else could I do? The ones they caught they sent to prison. This governor's a demon."

"I know. But it won't last forever. Better times are coming."

"May God hear you! I was desperate for a word of hope."

He inspected the surroundings, as if expecting a cop to appear at any moment.

"This city's no good anymore," he went on. "The poor, forced into hiding—how are we supposed to survive?"

"Don't be pessimistic," Heykal consoled him. "Come on, let's get out of here. Walk with me a bit; we can talk on the way."

The man seemed deeply afraid.

"I can't," he said. "They're everywhere. They're watching me."

"Don't be scared," said Heykal, taking him by the arm. "You're with me now. You can't be punished for walking with a friend."

"A friend!" exclaimed the beggar. "For saying that, I'd follow you to hell."

He set off with Heykal; at first he was hesitant, but soon he walked forthrightly by his side. Though his fear had apparently dissipated, he was still discreetly on guard. Heykal smiled; this encounter had pleased him. He was trying to think how he could help the beggar.

"Here's what I propose," he said at last. "There's no need for you to put yourself at risk by hanging around all the time waiting for me in the street. Come to my place once a month, and I'll give you everything then. That way, there's no risk."

Heykal glanced at the beggar, who looked sadder than ever. Clearly he wasn't at all satisfied by this proposition.

"What's the matter?" asked Heykal.

The man was quiet. He looked downcast, as if he'd just been deeply offended.

"I'm not your employee," he finally said. "What about our friendship? It's not just the money. I like talking to you—that's what I've missed the most."

"I understand," said Heykal. "I miss it, too. Still, you should do as I say." He pulled a coin from his pocket and slipped it into the beggar's hand. "Take this for now."

"May Allah make you prosper!" said the man. "It's done me good to see you; I feel a new hope growing in my heart."

Night had fallen. They arrived at the edge of a large, brightly lit square bordered by shops and cafés with crowded, noisy outdoor seating. In this high-security zone the beggar was overwhelmed by fear; he stopped, terrified, as if confronting a jungle of hungry wild beasts, and refused to go farther.

"So, do we have an understanding?" asked Heykal. "You'll come see me?"

"I'll come," the man promised. "To see you again, I would brave death! May Allah protect you."

Heykal warned him to be careful, then crossed the square.

The Globe was a pretentious café located on one of the most elegant streets of the European Quarter, not far from the cliff road. It was famous for its long stretch of open-air tables, before which passed a magnificent and unceasing parade of pretty girls. The majority of its customers—almost all, in fact—spent their time lustfully sizing up the feminine figures that sauntered by. The thin dresses worn by these divine creatures made the men's task as easy as it was mesmerizing. Some customers of the café—not the youngest—would sit and wait all day just to see the perfect curve of a beautiful leg or the quivering mystery of an anonymous haunch. And, in fact, the girls were as eager to display their charms as the men were to observe them; some of them were even said to go without underwear, just for the mischievous pleasure of watching the unfortunate voyeurs overheat. So at the Globe the outdoor tables were always full—except during the blistering midday hours, when it was customary for the young ladies to take their siesta. The inside of the café, however, was almost always empty—with the occasional exception of a pair of old codgers who, awaiting their departure for the sweet hereafter, played a lazy game of dominoes that would probably extend into the afterlife. Every now and then, roused despite themselves by the whoops from outside, they'd cast a dull glance through the window onto the objects of so much lust; then, faint with desire, they turned back to their senile game.

Heykal approached the café. He walked confidently, slipping between tables and carefully guarding the virgin purity of his magnificent, freshly ironed suit. He was looking straight ahead and seemed to pay no attention to the people in his path. He wondered if Khaled Omar was already there, and whether he would be recognized by him. Heykal wanted to gauge the intuition of his future friend and accomplice. It was a litmus test: surely any truly intelligent man would recognize him immediately! It seemed impossible that Khaled Omar—if he was the man Heykal imagined him to be—would fail to notice his presence.

Someone stood up in front of him, as if to block his way. It was Khaled Omar, a short man holding out a fat, ring-laden hand.

"What an honor to meet you!"

"The honor is all mine," responded Heykal. He pressed the businessman's hand.

"Please sit," said Khaled Omar.

Heykal sat. Khaled Omar remained standing for a few seconds, then sat as well. He gazed ecstatically at Heykal as if at an enchanting vision.

"Forgive me for making you wait," said Heykal. "Have you been here long?"

Khaled Omar emerged from his reverie.

"Ten minutes, if that, but it's nothing. I'm happy to see you. I recognized you right away."

The waiter approached. A glass of whiskey and a small plate of *loukoums* were already on the table.

"What can I get for you, bey?" asked the waiter, addressing Heykal.

Heykal ordered a whiskey, and the waiter left. Khaled Omar grabbed the plate of *loukoums* and offered it to the young man.

"Please, help yourself."

"No thanks," said Heykal, "not right now."

"Then forgive me for eating in front of you," said Khaled Omar. I adore sweets of all kinds."

He took a *loukoum* and popped it into his mouth, then licked the traces of powdered sugar from his fingertips.

Khaled Omar ate his *loukoum*, bobbing his head and gazing rapturously at Heykal.

"I recognized you right away."

"I have to admit that pleases me," responded Heykal.

"You were sure I would, weren't you?"

"What makes you think so?"

"Well, I thought it strange that you wanted to meet this way," said Khaled Omar. "I couldn't see why you'd want to make things difficult—our friend Karim could easily have introduced us. But in any case, his description of you didn't steer me wrong. I don't mean that he described the way you look or your clothes; no, he spoke only of your ideas. And that was enough for me to recognize you."

"So my ideas show on my face?" asked Heykal.

"It's hard to explain. I saw you walking across the square, and I said to myself: That's him. You had the look of someone who knows more than everyone else."

"I know two very simple things," Heykal said. "The rest is of no importance."

"I wonder if they're the same two things I know myself."

"I'm sure they are. It's why I'm here, and it's why we can speak frankly."

"So tell me what the first thing is. I'm listening."

Khaled Omar hastily re-knotted his tie and smoothed his well-groomed mustache with his fingers, as if whatever he was about to hear merited an impeccable appearance. There was a gleam of amusement in his eyes and a hint of anxiety on his face.

"Number one is that the world we live in is governed by the most revolting bunch of crooks to ever defile the soil of this planet."

"I couldn't agree more. And number two?"

"Number two is that you must never take them seriously, for that is exactly what they want."

"Agreed!" said Khaled Omar, and burst into a long, resounding laugh.

The laughter was contagious. As it spread to the surrounding tables, it grew even louder, outrageously loud. Khaled Omar turned from one neighbor to the next, winking as if to thank them for participating in his hilarity while encouraging their continued pursuit of such joyful delirium. Finally he got hold of himself; the others, however, were still convulsed with the mirth he'd so inconsiderately unleashed. Heykal had been unmoved by the general hilarity; he remained seated, stiff and aloof, observing his new friend with satisfaction. He was utterly delighted with this jovial little potbellied man, with his gleaming pomaded mustache and strong smell of violet-scented perfume. How unusual! A man whose success hadn't corrupted him one bit. He acted just as he had when he'd gone barefoot and even slept in the street. His bizarre outfit was only a disguise; all the riches in the world would never tame the crude joy and artless affability of his every gesture. His big, mocking laugh was an outright defiance launched in the face of power.

"You see?" Khaled continued. "There's all you need to know!"

"Yes," said Heykal. "But still, not enough people get it."

"Who cares? Don't tell me you're the kind who wants to make the world a better place?"

"God, no!" Heykal responded. "I have no interest in bettering anything. There's nothing worse than a reformer. They're all careerists."

"I thought you'd say that, but I'm relieved to hear it," said Khaled Omar. "I had the misfortune of encountering that kind in prison. They were no better than my jailers. So righteous—and as full of themselves as pregnant women. They made prison such a depressing place!"

"They're utterly tiresome," said Heykal, with something close to hatred. "All they want is to replace one government with another, ostensibly more-just one. They all dream of becoming ministers. Ministers! Can you imagine a filthier ambition! Please, I beg you, don't speak to me of those people!"

"You're right. So listen: I want to be clear about why I'm here. I'm

sure our friend Karim has told you how destiny magically trans-
formed me from a jailbird into a rich and respectable businessman.
A beautiful story—very instructive—and I'll tell it to you some day
in all its glorious detail because I know you'll appreciate it. But the
short version is I earned all my money in such a crazy, ridiculous
fashion that my eyes were opened to the madness of the world. Now
I'd like to put this money to use—in a way that isn't sensible or just.
I'd like to make a contribution to the madness of the world. Do you
understand?"

"Perfectly: a cause that is neither sensible nor just. I couldn't put
it better myself."

"It goes without saying that everything that is mine is yours. He
placed a brotherly hand on Heykal's arm. I'm eager to know: What
are your plans?"

Heykal remained silent. He wasn't surprised by the businessman's offer, it was just that something in his heart stirred whenever
he was reminded of his ability to sway others. This man, whom he
barely knew, had just offered him his fortune. What did he want in
return for such extravagance? This illiterate businessman was a
strange character indeed. What was it he'd said? To make a contribution to the madness of the world!

Heykal was almost scared to find so much lucidity in such an
unrefined mind. Had he just met his master? And what did Omar
want from him? What untold delights did he hope would result
from this mad pursuit to which he had just pledged his entire fortune? His entire fortune! That was more then Heykal had asked for.
As if it cost a fortune to entertain yourself! All you had to do was
look around: the spectacle was free.

Khaled Omar lifted his hand. His rings flashed, and the waiter
approached.

"Let's drink to our mutual understanding," said Heykal, raising
the glass the waiter had set down on the table.

Khaled Omar raised his own glass, and they toasted each other.

The street was packed with evening strollers enjoying the cooler
air at the end of the torrid day. There were the working stiffs, up-

right and formal; the dignified family men flanked by wives and children; the occasional pair of young newlyweds, who clutched each other's hands in a grotesque show of commitment. But none of the drinkers at the Globe paid any attention to this mundane procession. They weren't there to look at humanity in all its mediocrity; they were waiting for a luxuriantly curvaceous woman to show up and arouse their desire. From time to time a metallic squeal, sharp and deafening as a siren, signaled the ambling approach of a tram. The drivers of horse carts, who were so skilled at maneuvering through traffic jams, lashed out at the indolent mob filling the street, impervious to anything but the welcome sea breeze. Heykal tried in vain to locate a single bum, a single happy-go-lucky derelict who had managed to escape the clutches of the police. Not one. Reduced to the contributing members of society—in other words, the depressed and overworked—the city's streets were becoming strangely sinister. Wherever you went, you were surrounded by public servants. Heykal couldn't help but remember how the beggar had responded to his invitation to come collect his monthly sum at the house. That a starving beggar would refuse to be seen as an employee: what an insult to posterity, which only recognizes those who make careers of following the rules! History's full of these little bureaucrats who rise to high positions because of their diligence and perseverance in a life of crime. It was a painful thought: the only glorious men the human race had produced were a bunch of miserable officials who cared about nothing but their own advancement and were sometimes driven to massacre thousands of their own just to hold on to their jobs and keep food on the table. And this was who was held up for the respect and admiration of the crowd!

Khaled Omar waved away a fly that had landed on the plate of *loukoums* and gave Heykal a look full of unspoken expectation. Why was his companion so silent? Why was he pretending to be so interested in what was going on in the street? Was he having second thoughts? Khaled Omar had long imagined this meeting, and he'd wondered whether Heykal would ask for his help right off. Heykal's silence made him think he was hesitating to reveal his plans. This lack of confidence pained Omar. Hadn't he just put all his earthly goods at Heykal's disposal? The young man's visible coldness, the elegance of his manners, his wary sarcastic smile—none of this displeased Omar. They were the signs of an aristocratic mind. No, Khaled Omar admired Heykal without reservation. If only he'd deign to take his fortune and accept his devotion.

"Thank you for your generosity," said Heykal. "I will definitely need your help. But it won't cost a fortune. Much less."

"Whatever it is, give me your orders. I'm at your service."

Heykal crossed his legs and let his gaze stray over the passing crowd once more; then he turned to Khaled Omar and said:

"Well, I'm sure I don't need to tell you that the horror and stupidity of the current governor are completely beyond the pale."

"I know, and I also know that he's supported by a revolting clique of newspaper editors who can't stop singing his praises."

"That's not a bad thing. On the contrary: it'll make our task easier."

"How?"

"Very simple," said Heykal. "We're going to jump on the bandwagon. We, too, will sing the praises of our odious governor. We'll outdo them in their idiocy."

"Karim told me that the papers have stopped publishing your enthusiastic letters to the editor. Well, it was a magnificent idea! I want to congratulate you for it."

"That's all over. Now we're going to inaugurate an unprecedented campaign of subversive propaganda, the likes of which no secret police in the world has ever seen. For starters, I'll print posters featuring the governor's portrait with some words in his praise. The text will be so ridiculously laudatory, even the most naive citizens will laugh. With the help of some friends, we're going to put them up on every wall in the city. Do you understand the impact this will have?"

"Of course. Everyone in the city will think the governor had the posters printed to bolster his image."

"And why not! Has anyone ever known revolutionaries to attack a government with praise? Another thing: the governor himself will assume it's the work of some well-meaning supporters. He'll be flattered—that's for sure. He's too stupid to get it right away. But even if he did understand, it would be hard for him to take action against us. We'll go on soft-soaping him indefinitely—and what's the risk? They won't dare charge us with praising the governor too much—although I'll happily praise him in front of any tribunal. But it won't come to that."

"Your words fulfill my every hope!" said Khaled Omar. "By Allah, I don't know what to say!"

"And that's not all," Heykal went on. "These posters are only the beginning. I have other ideas. In a word, we're going to make the governor infamous across the country. He'll become such a laughingstock that the government will have to strip him of power."

Khaled Omar was wriggling in his seat, ever more captivated by his companion's diabolical perversity. And yet there was an important flaw in Heykal's logic. To plot the destruction of a man as entertaining as the governor: Wouldn't that work against their common desire? The thought silenced him momentarily.

"Let me ask you: Do you really want him to disappear?"

"To tell the truth, no. Where will we find a buffoon to match him? But in the end, unfortunately, we'll be forced to give him up. There'll be no choice."

"I'm getting the feeling," said Khaled Omar, "that I'm finally going to have some real fun."

A young goddess sailed toward the terrace, her breasts bobbing in her blouse like a ship on the high seas. Then, like a fleeting vision of debauchery, she was gone, leaving innumerable passions stranded in her wake. Right away the customers at a neighboring table started analyzing her beauty like real connoisseurs, and when they got to her rear end, it was as if they'd discovered the fundamental truth of the universe. A vigorous debate rich in imagery ensued, and no insult was spared when any disagreement arose in the course of their critique, which extended to the most intimate details of the unknown young woman's body.

"Women," said Heykal. "Aren't they enough for you?"

"I love women," responded Khaled Omar. "But they're nothing compared with the delights you propose."

"Are you married?"

"Of course. I'm a respectable businessman! But I should explain: It's not always the same model. I'm not one of those rich imbeciles who changes his car each year while keeping the same wife. Me, I change wives each year—and I don't even own a car."

"I'm happy for you," said Heykal.

"Sometimes I get rid of them even quicker. Women age faster than cars, believe me."

After a pause, he began again.

"Let's get back to business. What do you need from me?"

"What I need," said Heykal, "shouldn't be very difficult to find for a man with your resources. First I need a printing press, then a private place to do our work. Can you provide that?"

"Anything you wish. You'll have the printing press in two or three days at the latest. Isn't there anything else I can do?"

"That's all for now. Thank you. I'll take care of the rest."

"I assume you'll write the text for the poster?"

"No, not me. I'm going to ask one of my friends to do it. A schoolmaster named Urfy. Maybe you know him."

"I know him very well. I'm one of his students; I'm going to him to learn to read."

"You're going to Urfy's school!" exclaimed Heykal with genuine admiration. "My word! You're a remarkable man. Why do you want to learn to read?"

The businessman was tired of seeing Karim and his other literate friends laughing over articles in the papers. It demoralized him to feel so outside the loop. He had to beg them to read passages aloud. Once he'd been clued in, he could laugh too—even louder than the others—but this delayed satisfaction was tinged with bitterness. To end his dependency, he'd decided to learn to read; he wanted to be able to keep up with the delicious depravity of the ruling party all on his own.

"I wish I could really savor their lies. It's a pleasure I'm longing to experience. Unfortunately, I'm not making much progress. I'm a lousy student."

"Do you go regularly?"

"Oh, no! Only from time to time. I like Urfy a lot. Did you know that his mother's gone mad?"

"Yes, I knew that," said Heykal. "A few months ago she fell into a state of nervous prostration, a kind of gentle derangement. It could be much worse."

"Still, she's become a burden. He can't look after her and also attend to his students. Before she fell apart, she helped at the school; she was an educated woman. Believe me, our friend's situation is tragic, even though he won't admit it. Many times I've offered to pay for her care in a residential clinic that specializes in her kind of madness, but he always refuses. I'm afraid to go on insisting—I don't want to hurt his feelings. It's a delicate business. Couldn't you speak to him about it? With all my heart I want to help him, and I'm sure he'll listen to you."

Heykal had turned thoughtful. He'd known Urfy for a long time and knew all about the love and tenderness the schoolmaster felt for his mother. However crazy she got, he'd want to keep her close.

"I know Urfy very well. He's an eminently intelligent man. He claims that his mother isn't mad, that in this world to call someone mad is absurd. I think he makes perfect sense."

"I've heard that she still fills in for Urfy when he's away. Apparently the students don't notice a thing. They think she's just sick."

"It's very possible," said Heykal. "Personally, that's something I'd like to see."

Khaled Omar seemed taken aback by this display of cynicism.

"I can see that you're a man who lives according to his ideas. I like that."

"Why should there be a difference between a friend's madness and other people's?"

"I see what you mean," said Khaled Omar, exploding with laughter.

But this time, there was no corresponding echo from the surrounding tables. The customers all looked as if someone had died. For almost a quarter of an hour, not a single young woman had paraded before the tables.

# 6

A SMALL, distinct sound interrupted the silence that prevailed in the classroom. Urfy could identify it without lifting his eyes: one of the boys in the back was snacking on toasted watermelon seeds. Urfy had hesitated to intervene, not wanting to rouse the rest of the students, who—though momentarily subdued by the deadly midday heat—were apt to get excited about even the most minor occurrence. But the sound of the little brat gorging himself broke in on Urfy's concentration and inspiration. He was working on the text for the poster praising the governor, which Heykal planned to paste up all over the city. He seemed calm on the outside, but inside he was savoring this opportunity to compose an apologia for this important figure. As he shaped his masterpiece it came to resemble an epitaph, something for the tombstone of an illustrious hero. Urfy was so caught up in his role that he almost began to believe the inane compliments he was lavishing on the governor. With characteristic generosity, he'd given him every imaginable virtue, using language usually reserved by the newspapers only for notorious criminals, with one or more wars on their conscience.

Again the irritating noise: Urfy stopped in mid-sentence, raised his head, and decided it was time to put an end to this behavior, which was disrupting the sacred hours of siesta. A quick glance identified the guilty party. It was the redoubtable Zarta: a very bright ten-year-old boy who was also one of the most ingenious liars of the century—Urfy sometimes wondered whether he had a minister of the current government in his class. To unleash the devious powers of the boy might turn out to be a fatal error. Urfy knew the whole class was just waiting for a sign to awaken from its torpor, so he resigned himself to suffering through his student's obnoxious behavior. His desk was mounted on a platform, and he towered above the students: twenty boys and girls, aged six to ten, who'd been assigned the task of copying a list of words for common objects from the blackboard into their notebooks. Since the exercise was optional, most of them were dozing in their seats; in the stifling heat, they were in no mood for learning. Worn down and deflated, they let the flies devour their faces with impunity. Located in the basement of an old house, the classroom was a part of an apartment that Urfy shared with his mother. It was a fairly big room; a little daylight came in through the basement windows, which faced the sidewalk of a narrow commercial street. Most of the day, passing throngs of shoppers distracted the kids, who liked to shoot at their legs—the only visible part of them—with slingshots. But at this hour the street was empty; nobody would think of venturing out into this furnace.

Urfy took a handkerchief from his pocket and mopped his prematurely balding head. The bald spot was a mark of his professorial dignity; he never failed to groom and polish it well, like an expensive article of furniture in a poor person's home. It was a local belief that premature baldness indicated wisdom and knowledge, and Urfy liked to encourage this illusion, lifting his hand frequently to his pate—especially when faced with skeptical parents who had the audacity to treat him like a worthless young boy. But baldness wasn't the only physical mark of his genius: Urfy was also seriously-nearsighted. He wore steel-rimmed glasses with impressively thick lenses that magnified the severity of his discerning gaze. A bald schoolmaster afflicted with myopia—that was more than enough to inspire the confidence of an illiterate population that had been raised with the axiom that a blind man can do no harm.

Compared to the outside, the classroom was a cool oasis. Urfy loved the stillness of the afternoon, when the children, dazed by the heat, quieted down for once. He gave himself over to the pleasures of reflection. After years spent in the dusty offices of one government ministry or another, he'd finally found a profession that suited him. His generosity and the sweetness of his character had always led him to prefer the company of children to that of adults. Adults scared him: in each of them he saw a potential killer. Urfy needed to be able to love without an ulterior motive, without beating around the bush, without trickery, and, above all, with forgiveness. But how can you forgive an adult? Too much selfishness, foolishness, brutality, stymied hopes, and bitterness separated him from his contemporaries. And ambition! They were all racked with ambition. The wanted to make it! But make it where? And when they finally *had* made it—to the heights of glory or wealth—they turned into brutes: repugnant, arrogant monsters incapable of feeling the slightest human sentiment. What Urfy admired in children was, above all, their complete lack of ambition. They were content with their daily lot; they strove for nothing but the simple joys of being alive. But for how much longer? It passed quickly—childhood and the marvelous pointlessness of youth—an undeniable truth that filled Urfy with bitterness. These children would later become men. They would join the pack of wolves; they'd abandon their intransigent love of purity and lose themselves in the anonymous crowd of murderers.

One day he had the idea of opening a private school; it was a strike against the official system of education, which aimed to initiate children into the ignoble trickery of a society in decay. The system was an insult to the charmed, innocent dreams of childhood. For a long time Urfy had felt that if he ever did have something to say, he'd say it to children; he had no use for adults. So he lost no time putting his plan into action. With the consent of his mother, who would be assisting him, he freed up a room of their small basement lodgings, furnished it with a few benches and a blackboard, and then—to add a touch of seriousness to the enterprise—had a local painter make a majestic sign, which he hung above the door of the building. A handful of neighborhood families, tempted by the proximity of this hallowed hall of science (and even more so by the modest fee), enrolled their children before the paint on the sign was dry. And then something extraordinary happened. Against all expectations, the children manifestly adored their schoolmaster; they would kill their own parents before relinquishing their seats in this unlikely school. The parents—good, simple people who'd never imagined their offspring would exhibit such hunger for learning—were stunned. What they didn't understand was that at school their children inhabited an anarchic world that was perfectly to their liking, and that Urfy —despite his bald head and thick steel-rimmed glasses—was a dangerous practical joker. He spoke to his charges in a language that openly contradicted the language of adults. He inculcated them with a single principle: to know that everything grown-ups told them was false and that they should ignore it. So his classroom became a breeding ground for a generation of skeptics who honored no authority. Urfy was sometimes stunned by the unorthodox pronouncements that sprang to the children's lips.

Young Zarta's lousy manners were fully on display as he spat seed shells onto the classroom floor. This was too filthy for Urfy, who did the cleaning. It was time to intervene. In a quiet but firm voice, he said:

"Hey, kid! Go chew your seeds out on the street."

Zarta swallowed the seed he'd just crushed in his teeth and pretended to study the route of a fly that was circulating near the ceiling. Urfy took the ruler that hung from his desk and pointed it at the child.

"Hey, Zarta! I'm talking to you."

Seeing that he'd been found out, Zarta began to whimper—a pathetic sound that didn't fit his body, which resembled a well-fed pig. Zarta ate rapturously; he ate everything he could get his hands on, and by now he'd acquired a robust corpulence unusual for his age. He rose to respond.

"On the street, sir! In this heat! Do you want me to die?"

"Couldn't care less. Go on, scram!"

"But I was hungry, sir! I haven't eaten in three days."

"May Allah protect you," said Urfy, bowing his head. "What

would we do without you and your lies? But, sadly, you'll be leaving us soon; you're almost a man."

This insinuation by his schoolmaster struck Zarta as the ultimate betrayal. Trembling, he clutched at his stomach as if to quell an all-consuming hunger. He appeared to speak through tears:

"Why do you humiliate me, sir? What have I done to deserve this?"

The few students who'd been copying words from the board into their notebooks abandoned their noble endeavor; the rest woke up, yawning, and observed their classmate, who—proud of being singled out by the schoolmaster—groaned for appearance's sake and tried to look as hungry as possible.

"I'll tell you why you'll be leaving us," Urfy explained calmly. "First, because you're becoming fatter and fatter; second, because you lie like a rich man. It's distracting to have someone like you among us. Your lies are worth nothing here—it's time to go share them with the world. And now, stop gnawing those seeds. Go to sleep like your friends!"

"I'm not tired," whimpered Zarta, deeply upset at the prospect of leaving school. "But I promise to stop eating seeds. You've spoiled my appetite, sir!"

"Let's hope it's for good," said Urfy.

Some of the students began to reproach Zarta for having woken them for nothing; then they demanded fiercely that he share his seeds. It was turning into a bad scene. Urfy put a stop to this nascent offensive by pronouncing the magic formula he reserved for such cases:

"If you don't calm down, I'm going to kick you all out and close down the school!"

This threat, like a death sentence, produced the desired effect. Instantly the class fell silent, and Urfy was able to return to his text. He'd already finished, but he was enjoying fiddling with it, prettying up the sentences with outlandish adjectives and turns of phrase. Printed and posted on the city's walls, it would be worse than a price on the governor's head. Urfy was keenly sensitive to the subtlety of Heykal's maneuver: to put the terrible weapon of irony in the service of the revolution. Urfy acknowledged the power of irony and scorn. But for the last few months, an open wound in his heart had clouded his customary lucidity. He suffered from a pain that no dose of irony could alleviate: his mother had gone mad, becoming a caricature of a human being. He could not bring himself—dutiful son that he was—to appreciate the absurdity of this scary apparition, who, as a woman and mother, had been all sweetness and self-sacrifice. What good did it do to deny it? But seeing her now—the decrepit body, the pathetic face that seemed to sink deeper into darkness every day—he couldn't muster a laugh; he had no right. At some moments he gave up completely, relinquished the privilege of insight and fell back into the tormenting chaos that, from the beginning of time, has been pitted against it. Soon suffering would devour him whole. He'd lose his sense of humor, succumb to pessimism and unhappiness, and end up a truly miserable man, unable to teach the children he loved so much. He felt that he was betraying not just his own sensibility but also Heykal and his jovial crew. Because Heykal, though he maintained a strict silence on the subject, was not fooled. Nothing escaped the gentle authority of his gaze; it stripped away the useless trappings of the soul and enveloped it with proud love. There was no doubt in Urfy's mind: Heykal would have liked him to make a joke of his mother's madness. He was waiting, patient as the devil, for his friend to offer him this supreme proof; he anticipated it as a prodigious honor, a higher satisfaction. Why be upset, he seemed to be saying. Doesn't madness make the world go round? Whenever Urfy met Heykal he felt ashamed, like a traitor who knows he's been found out. It was ridiculous and demeaning, and it left Heykal looking brotherly and kind while Urfy sank into cruel confusion.

Footsteps resounded in the corridor and Urfy looked toward the back of the classroom. For a few seconds he remained frozen in an anxious state of expectation, dreading the inevitable appearance of his mother. But when he saw Karim instead, he smiled, relieved. The young man responded to his smile with a gesture that indicated he didn't want to disturb him and would wait to speak to him after class. Then, to be discreet, he tiptoed toward a school bench and sat down next to a young girl, whose red-tinted hair and orange dress made her look like an exotic fruit. She was very beautiful, and Karim liked to flirt with her.

The girl kept her eyes down and pretended not to notice his presence. Karim stroked her hair. He leaned in and murmured passionately in her ear:

"So, my love! Shall we give each other instructions?"

The girl didn't respond. Pouting, she turned her head as if a fly was bothering her.

"What is it?" Karim asked. "Are you breaking up with me or what? Answer me, oh my love!"

Without turning to him the girl said in a low and musical voice:

"Where are the presents you keep promising me, you liar?"

"Women!" lamented Karim with mock indignation. "Always so materialistic! And I thought you loved me for myself. Oh, how unhappy I am!"

He leaned on the desk, resting his forehead in his hand, and let out a series of deep sighs, all the while peering at the girl out of the corner of his eye. He waited to see what would happen. It didn't take long.

He felt the girl move, then touch his arm.

"But, I love you," she said in a whisper.

Karim silently rejoiced. Games of love like this made him happy. Whether they were seven or seventy, women always fell for the same tricks. Age didn't matter; you seduced them all the same way. He stroked the girl's hair lightly, a tender gesture of reconciliation, and looked around the class. How marvelous to be sitting at a school

desk again: suddenly he felt the desire to act like a student. He grabbed the girl's notebook and, writing meticulously, began to translate a popular proverb about human ingratitude: "We are the ones who taught them to beg, and now they beat us to our own benefactors' doors." Karim copied the sentence several times, as devoted as a star student. He'd forgotten his age and the absurdity of his presence here. All he wanted was to shine. The girl watched him, captivated; she'd never seen such a serious student.

There was still a quarter of an hour left before the end of class, but Urfy cut the session short.

"All right, children, be off!"

"But it's not time yet, sir!" protested several students, waking up with a jolt.

"No protests," interrupted Urfy. "I've seen enough of you for today."

With heavy hearts, dragging their feet as much as they could, the children succeeded in gathering all their belongings and left the classroom. But they didn't go far; they just scattered into the narrow street, searching for dark corners not too far from the school. When the last student had left, Urfy stepped down from his desk and went over to Karim, who hadn't budged from his seat.

"I didn't expect you so early," he said, by way of an excuse.

"I had nothing else to do," Karim admitted. "And I couldn't wait to read what you'd written. You've finished, I hope?"

"Just," responded Urfy. He pulled a folded piece of paper from the inside pocket of his jacket and offered it to Karim: "Here, read."

"You're happy with it?"

"That's a question to ask His Excellency the Governor. I am but his humble biographer."

Wanting to indulge fully in the delight he anticipated from this reading, Karim assumed a comfortable position. Then he unfolded the paper, and what he read made him almost crazy with pleasure. A storm raged within him, it seemed, making him shake with insane, unstoppable laughter. Urfy hadn't expected such a success; he was passably proud of the text but was still surprised. Some of the children, overhearing this bout of hilarity, crept out of the shadows of the nearby houses and spied on them through the basement windows. Seeing the beardless wonders preparing to jeer at them, Karim calmed down immediately. He wiped the tears from his cheeks and turned to the schoolmaster.

"It's ... sublimely grotesque," he said, jubilation in check. "With the portrait above it, this will make a sensational poster!"

"Do you really like it?" asked Urfy.

"It's ... well ... monstrous! I can't wait to print it."

"That's your domain. But tell me: How do you know about printing?"

"By chance. I worked for a few months as a typesetter in a print-shop. It was during the time when I wanted to live among the people. So I took different jobs."

Urfy slumped onto a bench and stretched his legs, which were numb from inactivity. His gaze fell on his worn-out shoes, and he noticed something strange: one was more worn than the other. Briefly the mystery absorbed his mind, then he snapped back to attention and placed his hand fraternally on the young man's shoulder.

"You were very young," he said, "and you wanted to defend the cause of the people, is that it? And you got sent to prison."

Urfy wasn't asking a question but stating a simple fact. Everyone knew that defending the cause of the people led straight to jail.

"Naturally," responded Karim. "Not that I regret it, because at the end of the day, it was in prison that I did get to mix with the people. See, in a factory you slave away like beasts—there's never time to talk to your co-workers. All your conversations come back to the job, the awful pay, or the contagious misery that tears families apart. Nothing but painful subjects. But in prison there is down-time; you talk for the pleasure of getting to know one another. It's funny, but a prison is less sinister than any workplace. Do you know that before prison I believed that 'the people' were sullen by nature and were somehow predisposed to misery and hardship? I never would have believed they were so lively, so full of humor. Yes, it was only in prison that I discovered this fundamental truth about our people—and realized that all my ideas about them had been false."

Like any intellectual worthy of the name, Urfy had also fought for the people in his youth. But his unassuming air, his shyness and fear of attracting attention made him all but invisible to the police, who cared more about revolutionary looks than about actual revolutionary fervor. As a result, he'd never gone to jail. Now his curiosity was piqued; he realized he could learn from Karim's experiences. He pressed Karim's shoulder, encouraging him to continue.

"Tell me about it."

"Well," resumed Karim, "I'd seen the people as I'd wanted to see them, consumed by hatred and dreaming of revenge. And I wanted to help them carry out that revenge. I thought they were oppressed—but then I realized they were freer than I was. You wouldn't believe how they laughed when I tried to explain that I was in prison because of my political ideas. It was a disaster; they thought I was an idiot. And I thought that by announcing my revolutionary position—how I was declared an enemy of the government—I'd earn their respect! How presumptuous! They'd always known that the government was a joke. But with all of my intelligence, I'd taken it seriously! I felt like an ass, playing the martyr to the working class. I was the only one who took the government seriously."

"What a blow to your ego!" Urfy observed. "I bet you weren't happy about it."

"At first, no. But then my position began to seem silly. Soon I was laughing at everything, too, and in the end I was converted. And there was plenty to laugh about, believe me. It's amazing the different characters you meet in prison! Their ideas about the government were fantastic—it was nothing more than a bunch of perverts. I loved everything I heard."

"So prison was a decisive experience for you."

"It was a start. And then I met Heykal."

At the mention of Heykal, Urfy flinched. He withdrew his hand from the younger man's shoulder and went back to contemplating his worn-out shoes. He thought of the pleasure Heykal must have felt hearing Karim talk about his time in prison; it was a story that would feed right into his endless appetite for the ironic. Urfy refused to be seduced by the strange buffoonery of the world; he actually fought against the temptation of enjoying it too much. He was well aware that the world was ruled by idiots and crooks who deserved no respect, but this gave him no pleasure; instead, he felt the full bitterness of the situation. Unlike Heykal, he would try at times to find a semblance of sincerity or justice in human institutions. Sadly, facts always proved Heykal right—he triumphed at every turn. And it wasn't just that he triumphed; he shocked Urfy with his mania for seeking out the sick, risible side of every activity—as if to find the slightest grain of sanity in the whole comic routine might spoil his happiness. But Urfy was often incensed. In spite of everything he held on to a vague hope, and this condemned him to moral isolation from his friends—men whom he loved and admired.

"So," he finally said, "tonight's the night? You'll be able to do it?"

"I'll print enough," Karim said, "for us to start postering tonight. But we should get going. I'll need your help—to correct the proofs at least."

"Where's the printshop?"

"In a warehouse near the port that belongs to Khaled Omar. He should be coming with Heykal to meet us there this evening."

"So Heykal's coming?"

"For sure. He has to give us his final instructions. Did you know this is only the beginning, that Heykal has other projects in mind? Just thinking about it keeps me up at night!"

Karim's enthusiasm for Heykal's genius prevented him from noticing the look of sadness on the schoolmaster's face. Karim was so happy to be caught up in the whole giant hoax that nothing else seemed to matter.

"There are things about him I don't really understand," said Urfy.

"Who are you talking about?"

"I'm talking about Heykal. Listen to me: these posters—I'm the first to recognize their destructive power. But I wonder if Heykal really wants to take down the governor. I wonder if, to be happy, Heykal doesn't actually need the governor. What do you think?"

"What do we care if the governor's taken down or not? That's no business of ours. We just want to have fun—isn't that right?"

"I'm sorry, Karim, my brother, but sometimes I just forget to laugh. It's a weakness, I know, but I can't help it."

Though he wasn't going to let himself think about it, Karim was fully aware of the troubles that weighed on the schoolmaster's sensitive soul. To have a mother who'd gone crazy was hardly cause for celebration. Karim understood this so well, in fact, that he'd do anything to avoid the woman; she terrified him. When he came to see Urfy, he went out of his way not to cross her path. Now suddenly he felt she was there, spying on them, and he flinched as if at the approach of danger. Despite himself, he turned toward the door. He didn't see anyone at first; then the crazy old lady materialized before his eyes. There she was, towering in the doorframe like a specter—an old lady reduced almost to a skeleton but with a mysterious, bewitching power. She looked haggard and disheveled. She'd stopped eating a long time ago and now only nibbled at bread crumbs while staunchly refusing anything of substance. Eyeing the empty classroom with its deserted seats, she deliberately ignored her son and the stranger who was with him. At first Karim was petrified; he thought he was seeing a ghost. But then, robotically, he rose and bowed deeply to the emaciated form in the doorway.

Urfy had remained calm. He gestured to Karim to keep still and looked up at the strange apparition, his myopic eyes moist with emotion.

Full of confidence, propelled by an ancient reflex of maternal authority, the old woman strode toward them. Karim thought of running, but it was too late. He no longer felt like laughing, that was sure.

"Where are the children?" asked the woman. "He's the only one left," she added, looking at Karim with suspicion.

"Mother," said Urfy. "You don't recognize my friend Karim?"

"Of course I recognize him. He's a good student, he'll succeed in life. Since the others have left, he'll recite his lesson for me."

She walked briskly to the platform and sat down at Urfy's desk, resolute. With a bony hand she picked up the ruler, pointing it at Karim:

"Well then, young man! Recite your lesson!"

Karim was in hell. He glared at Urfy with the desperate look of a drowning man who loves life and dreads dying. But Urfy paid no attention to his distress—he had assumed an impenetrable mask and was following the scene with the cold assurance of a psychiatrist observing a hypothesis play out. The schoolmaster's attitude troubled Karim. Was this some kind of revenge, leaving him at the mercy of a madwoman? Was Urfy expecting him to explode into laughter, as he usually did no matter the situation? Yes, it was a dare: that and nothing else.

Finally, at the end of what seemed to be an eternity, Urfy spoke in a matter-of-fact tone without any urgency:

"Mother, it's time for you to go to bed."

The old lady didn't seem to hear; she was sticking to her idea.

"Come on, child! You're holding us up!"

Karim realized that to escape from this trap, he'd have to play along with her game. Remembering a vaguely patriotic text that he'd learned in his childhood, he started to recite it in a hoarse voice, clearing his throat several times in the process.

The madwoman watched him with her demented eyes; she seemed to be enjoying his recitation. Despite her witchlike demeanor, she still projected the prim dignity of a schoolmistress on a mission.

"That's very good," she said when Karim had finished. "I congratulate you! You've made progress since the last time. I'll tell your father that you are deserving of the money he spends on you."

Karim bowed deeply from the waist several times, as if the congratulations of the old lady were too heavy for his humility to bear. Deep down, he felt intensely proud of his triumph over the circumstance. He grinned victoriously at Urfy, showing that he'd taken note of his challenge and had risen to it handsomely.

Just then, Urfy was seized by panic. All of a sudden he couldn't see—he thought he'd been struck blind. It took him a moment to understand the reason for this sudden loss of sight: the tears he'd been struggling to repress now filled his eyes, and the lenses of his glasses were all fogged up. He removed them quickly and wiped them off with his handkerchief, his fingers shaking with panic. When he put them back on, he saw that the two protagonists of his nightmare were still in place, immobile, dumbstruck as if waiting for him—and him alone—to break off the session. He hurried to the podium, put his arm around his mother's shoulders, and all but carried her to the door. The madwoman let him do as he pleased, oblivious now to everything; she didn't even give a passing glance at Karim. He bowed one last time and didn't straighten up until they had left the room.

He wasn't alone for long. Urfy returned right away, deeply troubled.

"Please excuse me," he said, in a quiet voice. "I'm terribly, terribly sorry!"

Now that the danger was past, Karim was as jovial as ever.

"No harm done," he remarked cheerfully. He was going to add "It was a real pleasure," but restrained himself in time.

"It's my fault," Urfy went on. "I should confine her to her room, but I don't have the heart to do it."

"Don't feel bad," said Karim. "You know, for me it was a magnificent surprise! I never could recite that lesson when I was a kid, and look how it came back all of a sudden! It's amazing, don't you think?"

Urfy didn't feel like responding; all he said was:

"Shall we go?"

# 7

EMERGING from the basement into the blazing street, they felt a blast of intense heat and immediately began to sweat. Karim took off his jacket and draped it over his arm; then he unbuttoned his collar and rolled up his sleeves, taking on a sporty look. Urfy didn't follow his friend's sartorial lead; too many of his students' parents were around for him to indulge in such informality. Keeping their distance from each other—the slightest touch would be unbearable in this atmosphere—they walked toward the port. On the way they passed an infinity of empty side streets where, inside the rare open shops, you could see the owners taking their siestas in their chairs, handkerchiefs draped across their faces to ward off flies. They looked so much like corpses that Karim had to look away with a shudder. Farther on, half-naked children played in the puddles left by the municipal sprinklers; they splashed around happily and peppered Karim with insults as unoriginal as the minds of their mothers. The young man sighed: this generation had no talent for invective, a weakness he attributed to the new regime. But the heat distracted him from this distressing thought. In a hurry to escape from the furnace he picked up his pace, dragging Urfy in his wake.

Twenty minutes into this feverish walk they started to feel a slight breeze, a sign they were nearing the sea. Between buildings they glimpsed long ocean liners, anchored and at rest. Karim stopped in front of a run-down yellow building, took a key from his pocket, and opened the padlock on the immense double-hung gate.

"Come in," he said to Urfy.

The warehouse Khaled Omar had loaned them contained immense amounts of all kinds of merchandise; countless crates and sacks were stacked against the walls and rose from the dirt floor to the ceiling. They'd had to clear the middle of the space to set up the manual press, whose metal frame gleamed faintly in the dim light. The cleared area was not very big, and Urfy got the impression that the crates might all come tumbling down onto his head. He picked his way carefully, eyes focused on the one small, grilled window that let in a stingy stream of light. After the blinding glare of the street, this was all he had to guide himself by in the darkness. When he reached the window, he saw that someone had set up a table and two chairs. On the table were trays full of lead type. Taking a seat, he mopped his forehead with his handkerchief and gazed with wonder at the great metal machine enthroned there like a fantastic beast in a jungle of merchandise.

Karim bustled around the press like a child getting ready to show off a complicated toy. He turned toward Urfy.

"Superb, isn't it?" he said with the pride of ownership. "It's almost new. Khaled Omar has demonstrated his sincerity; he spared no expense."

"Yes," said Urfy. "Will you tell me what you need me to do?"

"In a minute, we'll start setting type. I'll explain how it works; it's not hard. But first let's turn on some lights—I can't see anything in here."

He went to flip the switch. Two bare lightbulbs suspended from the ceiling projected a harsh light into the room, reintroducing a dim hint of the blazing heat outside.

"Let's get started," said Karim, going over to the table and sitting down in the other chair.

"At your service," Urfy said.

By nine that evening, when Heykal arrived with Khaled Omar, more than five hundred posters bearing the portrait of the governor in full military dress were piled on the floor of the warehouse. The businessman wore a bottle-green suit and a dazzling red tie, and smelled more strongly than ever of violets. He walked up to Karim and took the young man in his arms, kissing him on both cheeks and showering him with congratulations. At the late hour his exclamations rang out and echoed throughout the silent port.

"You've done all this already! What a genius!"


Khaled Omar fell silent as Heykal began to read the poster out loud, articulating each word as solemnly as a death sentence. Hearing the litany of praise for the governor, Khaled Omar could hardly contain his joy: he bobbed his head like an imbecile; he clutched his chest as if suffocating with happiness. But, in fact, he was just coming to a full appreciation of the murderous treachery of their hoax and was congratulating himself for his part in it.

"The portrait alone is eloquent enough," said Heykal, when he'd finished his reading. "But I bow down before the writer; he's just caused the suicide of our beloved governor."

And for the first time since he'd entered the warehouse, he looked at Urfy.

Urfy received the compliment with some embarrassment, as if his inability to fully share Heykal's pleasure made him guilty, a traitor to his cause. He smiled appreciatively, but Heykal seemed to detect the bitterness behind the smile. He became very serious, then, after a moment's reflection, he addressed the schoolmaster again.

"You know how much I love you, brother. But there's something about you that's making me worry. Are you ill? That would upset me deeply."

He spoke with such sincerity that Urfy was both moved and disturbed. But he recovered quickly, realizing what Heykal was alluding to by inquiring after his health. He was asking, indirectly, for news of his mother—his unfortunate mother, his private affliction. Heykal couldn't hide his real intentions; Urfy had seen him in action too many times. Every time he came over, he would visit the old lady's room; you'd think he came just to see her. Then with the same serious look he had at this moment, he'd speak to her, displaying his most refined manners and putting on his best gentlemanly tone. And, incredibly, the madwoman was flattered; she grew coquettish; she called him "prince." It was an unnerving spectacle—Urfy couldn't understand how it worked, and he preferred to forget it once it was done. He wondered if Heykal only responded to the crazy side of life and if he wasn't a bit crazy himself.

"I'm doing very well," he replied.

"But you look tired," Heykal observed.

"I'm very busy these days. You know, I'm the sole director of the school."

"I understand. But why the bitterness? My dear Urfy, you know how much I care about you. I'd hate for anything to come between us."

"What bitterness?"

"Your behavior has changed. It's as if you don't agree with us anymore. Don't you like our new projects?"

"I share your ideas entirely," said Urfy with the vigor of a disciple accused of lack of enthusiasm. "If I'm bitter, it's nothing to do with our projects. It's personal."

"Well then, listen to me. When these posters are plastered on the walls of this city, people will be stunned—they won't know what to think. Even the regime will wonder if it's a publicity stunt pulled by the governor. There'll be terrible confusion. And it makes no sense to stop there. We'll put up posters in every corner of the city, and after, we'll put up others. Starting now, we are all devotees in the cult of the governor—even in casual conversation. Can I count on you?"

But Urfy didn't have the time to respond. Suddenly they heard the booming laugh of Khaled Omar, who was lounging in a chair while listening to Karim read from the poster. The businessman couldn't get enough of the panegyric; he asked his young friend to read it again right away, which Karim did. Urfy looked at Karim and

thought of the scene at the school between the young man and his mother. He was overcome with shame. Would Karim tell Heykal? Of course, he'd brag about it as a victory. The thought chilled Urfy's heart. He felt no rancor toward Heykal, only regret at not being able to love him unconditionally. He admired Heykal; he could sacrifice his life for such a man. Heykal with his impeccable appearance and his aristocratic manners was always the same; personal problems could never rattle his cold determination. Urfy envied him this sheer indifference to unhappiness. He felt alone, attached by a thread to Heykal's madcap world. Would the thread break?

"Everything's ready for tonight?" Heykal asked Karim.

"Yes, everything's ready," Karim replied. "I made an appointment with some friends and they're supposed to join me here soon. We'll form groups and divvy up the neighborhoods."

"Excellent. You've been wonderful!"

"When I think about the posters I pasted up a few years ago, attacking the government..."

"And now you're praising it. What a nice change!"

"I'll come along," Khaled Omar proposed. "I want to put up at least one."

"Not a good idea," said Heykal.

He didn't say why, but he was thinking that Khaled Omar's wild getup and booming laugh would attract attention to the group.

"I bow to your orders," said the businessman, not in the least put out.

Heykal smiled at him. Then said:

"You must excuse me—I have to go."

He walked over to the pile of posters and took one, stared at it for a while, then folded it up and slipped it into the breast pocket of his jacket.

"I might need it tonight," he said enigmatically. "Goodbye!"

He left the warehouse and walked out into the empty street, happily inhaling the invigorating scent of the sea.

# 8

THE SCENT of the sea mingled with the perfume with which
Soad had doused her wispy, half-developed adolescent body. She
rolled on the sand, striking lewd poses as if to seduce the stars; no
one else was in sight. She was on the beach at the end of the deserted
casino promenade, in a sheltered spot away from the twinkling lights
of the open-air disco. By the time it reached her, the music's deafening beat had died down, acquiring a ghostly resonance as ethereal as
her own presence on this abandoned stretch of sand. She froze for
an instant, her face set in a childish pout; then she scooped up a fist-
ful of sand and let it sift over her hips, enjoying the sensation of it
pressing down on her, heavier and heavier, massaging her like a deep
caress. She repeated this trick a few more times, hovering on the
brink of ecstasy, resisting the desire that flooded through her body.
Suddenly she stopped; with a supple flick of the hips, she shook the
sand from her dress and turned to look at the lights of the disco.

The world at the end of the deserted promenade looked eerie and
vaguely fantastical: she could have been watching the scene from a
planet thousands of kilometers away. On the dance floor, surrounded by greenery, fountains, and dwarf palms, couples moved
like marionettes controlled by a madman. She saw her father sitting
in the governor's box, separated by a railing from the rest of the
guests. The governor was holding court before her father, two men
she didn't recognize (they did nothing but nod their heads in a sign
of agreement), and a well-known singer, who according to rumor

had been the governor's mistress for the last several months. Her name was Om Khaldoun, and she was old, fat, and as hideously made-up as a pharaoh's mummy; she'd escaped ruin thanks to the narcissism of certain men of standing in the city. To be the lover of a famous singer was a chance to show off their fortune—the word was that she charged these archaeologists of the flesh a pretty penny. Every time she saw Om Khaldoun, Soad wondered how any man—however philistine and lacking in aesthetic sensibility—could make love to such a withering, flabby creature for vanity alone. Once the singer had been her father's mistress, and the girl still held painful memories of the time. That was when her hatred for her father grew into insurmountable disgust; she wouldn't let him near her anymore, let alone touch her. He seemed contagious to her; he exuded the stench of old lady, like the stench of rot. Even after he broke things off with the singer, it was a long time before the girl could look at him without repulsion.

Soad's father epitomized the greedy, power-hungry bourgeoisie who reigned over the city like a pack of jackals ripping into a carcass. He restricted his associations to his own kind—but only the more servile among them, people he could lord it over and put down as he pleased. He was insolent, disdainful—even with the governor. Soad, powerless and mortified, had listened for years as her father cut people down with the precision of an executioner. Nothing escaped his peremptory judgments or his furious condescending outbursts. These usually happened in the middle of the receptions he hosted in his sumptuous villa, as vast as a palace and swarming with servants. He'd start by welcoming his guests as if their very arrival was a humiliation to be avenged as soon as possible. Then, after shaming his visitors, he'd stir up bitter arguments about business and politics. Nobody dared contradict him: the virulence of his rejoinders was legendary. His way of carrying on a conversation—he would submit his interlocutor to a stream of scathing invective—attracted the city's elite in droves; each came to see the others insulted. But his daughter he treated with a careful, almost timid benevolence. Her rebellious temperament frightened him; he suspected that a full-scale revolt was in the making. All he asked was for her not to cause a scandal. That was what panicked him: scandal. He trembled at the thought of her getting pregnant, dreading the prospect like nothing else. And Soad knew it; every day she could see him staring at her stomach, as if expecting to see it swell with that terrible scandal. But having settled on this obsession, he paid no further attention; apart from that, he knew nothing about her.

Heykal's silhouette emerged from the lights of the disco, and she watched him walk toward her on the promenade, long and slim and superb, like an enigmatic god emerging from the void. She leaped to her feet but didn't run toward him; she waited valiantly until he was in front of her before throwing her arms around his neck and hanging from him, bouncing up and down and sighing hugely and happily, like a child who has been given a fantastic toy and can't believe her luck. He endured her caresses with tender indulgence. He was susceptible to these signs of adoration, to the rush of inarticulate words like the babbling of a drowning victim come back to life—in short, the frenzied behavior of a young girl in love. She continued kissing him and rubbing up against him, shameless in her desire, clearly hoping to lure him onto the sand. Finally Heykal freed himself from her clutches and pulled away gently.

"All right, little girl, that's enough for now," he said.

"You're so mean to me," she moaned.

She was distraught, on the verge of tears, pouting like a child who's been mistreated by an adult. But it was an act, a way of playing the victim to get his sympathy. She never knew if he was happy to see her or not. He never told her he loved her. He was always impassive, even in the throes of passion, with the same wry smile on his lips, the same expression of bottomless pride—not so much remote as willful and controlling.

"You really are mean to me," she said again, pounding at his chest with her fists.

Heykal laughed.

"Come now, let's stop the theatrics," he said, taking her by the arm and escorting her along the beach.

The truth was, he didn't want to make love to her there because he was afraid of ruining his clothes. He had to be in the casino soon, on a mission requiring utmost discretion; an unkempt outfit would make him stand out. And at the moment, anyway, he felt an excitement that was quite different from carnal desire as he contemplated the web he had woven for the governor and the inevitable repercussions of the postering campaign.

They stopped where the casino's private beach had been roped off. Soad sat on the rope pretending to swing. Heykal remained standing, looking at her, then sat down next to her and put his arm around her waist. From here the darkness seemed infinitely opaque; the only light was the glimmer of the stars reflected in the sea. The music had stopped, and with the sudden silence the faintly glowing buildings of the casino were plunged into a catastrophic remoteness. Heykal felt they were the only survivors in an annihilated world; suddenly possessed by a strange feeling of power, he pulled Soad firmly and desperately to him, as if to defend her even from death.

Then he let go and asked:

"Is your father here?"

"Yes, he's with the governor. How'd it go tonight?"

"Very well. The posters will be up by tomorrow morning. The portrait of the governor is so good it's frightening; it's even more lethal than the accompanying text. What I'd like is for you to pay close attention to the governor's reaction. Do your best!"

"That's all I am to you, a spy," she said, pouting. "You're so cruel!"

It was partially true; Soad had often spied on the governor when he met with her father. The governor still thought of her as a young girl and had no qualms about divulging official secrets in her presence. There was a time when the two men's conversations made the young girl yawn. She found it dull to hear them go on about such stupefyingly serious matters of state. But ever since she'd known Heykal, she'd become quite curious about all the things that the governor, thanks to his studied stupidity, carelessly let slip. Whenever she could (and it was to amuse herself as much as to please him), she'd report back to Heykal, revealing the details of the governor's plots and plans.

She got up and stood before him imploring:

"Do you love me?"

Coming from the mouth of a little girl this banal question was especially poignant. Heykal felt sobered; he wouldn't allow himself to be sucked down into love's murky waters. What he felt for her was nothing like the ferocious passion she seemed to harbor for him. She mistook the real and incomparable complicity that bound them together for a mere sentimental bond, made up of nothing but platitudes and habit. But how could he explain the difference to her? She had no idea, and it would be cruel for him to disabuse her. She was a woman, after all, and he couldn't ask her to deny her nature.

"Of course I love you," he responded with a bitter, pained smile—smiling not at the lie but at the sadness he already felt knowing he'd lose her someday.

"What a man I have!" she cried out, thrilled. "The fact that a man like you even exists is a miracle!"

In her delight she jumped off the rope onto the sand, but Heykal grabbed her and made her sit next to him again. Then, caressing the back of her neck, he said:

"Listen, I have a job for you. The next time you come to see me, bring a typewriter. I'll dictate a letter to you."

"What are you plotting now? A new hoax?"

"Well, yes. I'm going to send a letter to all the papers asking them to set up a subscription to pay for a statue of the governor."

Soad clapped her hands at the announcement of this plan; again she tried to stand up, wanting to demonstrate her enthusiasm, but Heykal held her down firmly and ordered her to remain calm.

"Listen," he went on, "that's not all. You've got a part to play in this. Do you know who's going to sign this letter? Your father, the most eminent of the governor's friends."

"What a devil! How I love you!" She threw her arms around his neck and covered his face in tiny kisses.

"And I'll need to see your father's signature in order to imitate it. Can you get me one?"

"That's easy. I'll have him write me a check. It won't be the first time—that's how he gives me money."

"Excellent!" exclaimed Heykal. "I'm so proud! Ask him for a check made out to cash so I can include it with one of the letters. I'll send that one to the most influential paper—it'll make the letter all the more believable. After that, the rest of the papers will publish the letter without question."

Soad suddenly doubled over, screeching with vicious laughter—the laughter of a woman scorned, seeking revenge.

"Ah! what a fool! If he only knew!"

"Who?" said Heykal.

"My father. Do you think he'll commit suicide? Oh, I hope he does, I hope he does!"

"Your personal problems don't interest me," Heykal said. "You must understand that."

The fierce hatred in the girl's laugh reminded Heykal once again of the abyss between them. Women loved deliriously, but they hated with the violence of an unchained beast. And hatred was an emotion that Heykal lacked completely. His profound distrust of humanity in general made him loathe to dignify with his hate the buffoons who strutted around on the world's stage, proudly proclaiming their crimes. He looked at the girl's disappointed face; she seemed to be waiting for a word or a caress from him to renew her spirits. But he was silent. He was thinking about another face, a face of extraordinary serenity in which hatred had been abolished forever. All the tenderness in him went out toward the face of the old madwoman, Urfy's mother. Her insanity was what he admired more than anything; she existed on a plane free of corruption, an extraterrestrial universe of inviolable purity, immune to the usual abominations. Heykal, who cared about nothing, was jealous of Urfy's crazy mother, this sublime being buried in a basement in an unsavory part of town; the schoolmaster possessed the one thing that could actually move Heykal. He had to hide it from Urfy, painfully aware as he was that his friend would never understand such a special veneration. He knew that Urfy secretly reproached him for his frequent visits to the old woman's room, that he suspected him of a diabolical regard for his mother. How could he know that these were Heykal's only moments of true feeling, when his devotion and kindness flowed freely and he was capable, at last, of boundless self-sacrifice? Faced with this old madwoman, a human reject, he was blinded by tears of tenderness and love. But he would rather endure Urfy's terrible suspicions than confess to the infinite sweetness of those moments when he gave in to the force of that sad face. The situation was awkward, and it troubled him so much that he'd greatly reduced the frequency of his visits to the old lady. Now just the thought of her face—like a martyred child's—could trigger the tremor in his soul that had become indispensable to his happiness.

There was a hint of unrest in Heykal's silence, and Soad instinctively picked up on it. She fidgeted on the rope, sighing, anxious for him to come back to her. The music picked up again in the distance, bright and clear in the night.

"Why don't we go dance," she finally said. "My father is busy with the governor, he won't notice a thing. It's been so long since I've danced with you."

"No, it's impossible," said Heykal. "Go back to your father. I've got to go to the casino."

"Will I see you after?"

"I'll come to the disco—but not for long. I have things to do to-night."

"I know what you have to do." She glanced at him with complicity and added a tragic pout.

"Don't be jealous," said Heykal, laughing.

"I'm not jealous now. But I warn you, I will be when I'm older."

"But you're already old enough," said Heykal, teasing her. "You're almost seventeen!"

"Dirty old man!"

She was going to whimper again, but Heykal got up to leave. Soad flung herself at him, slapping him and trying to kiss him at the same time. With consummate skill—and a battery of false promises—he managed to disentangle himself. Then he crossed the promenade and turned left, toward the casino.

It was a stucco building, adorned with mosaics, architecturally reminiscent of an opulent Hindu tomb. Heykal entered the room with the quick, irreverent step of a gambler who can't wait to bet the house. An intense, oppressive, almost agonized silence greeted him. He'd arrived at the critical moment: the croupier had just thrown the ball onto the roulette wheel. It rattled around, struggling like a trapped mouse, and the sound filled the room. The atmosphere was feverish, the heat suffocating; no breeze came in through the enormous picture windows with their panoramic view of the sea. Heykal walked past the groups of gamblers glued to the edges of the long table, but nobody turned—even an earthquake couldn't have wrested their concentration from the wheel. The ball went on rattling as Heykal made his way to the rear of the room where a ramp led from the side of an immense bar back to the bathrooms. The men's room was empty. Heykal held his ear to the door to make sure nobody had followed him down the corridor; no footsteps, just a muffled rumble in the distance—the ball must have finally landed, releasing the gamblers from their agony. The moment seemed right for him to go to work. He pulled the poster from his pocket, slapped glue on the wall above the urinals, and quickly put it up; now the governor would get to see all the casino's clients unzip. It was simply fantastic! Heykal stood back to admire his masterpiece. He was still savoring it with malicious delight when he heard the sound of footsteps in the corridor. This complicated things: for him to be seen would inevitably arouse suspicion. And if it was someone he knew, he'd be hard-pressed to avoid a conversation that might drag on dangerously. The light switch was within reach; he flipped it, plunging the bathroom into darkness, and slipped behind the door. The footsteps, heavy and ungainly, came closer, and a man entered the bathroom. The pale light from the corridor revealed an enormous mass stumbling toward the urinal, a middle-aged man, very fat, and, at first glance, unfamiliar to Heykal. He was mumbling indistinctly and must be very drunk. Heykal stood still, holding his breath. He didn't dare move yet; he was waiting for the man to start urinating so he might escape unnoticed. The man had turned his back and spread his legs, his massive silhouette cut out against the background of white tile; he seemed to be struggling with his fly. He was drunk enough not to be bothered by the lack of light, and Heykal was about to hand it to himself when the man began to sputter complaints about the casino management. He leaned over—with surprising agility, given his condition—to the light switch; there was a click, and the brightness returned. Before Heykal could make a move, the man saw the portrait of the governor on the wall. After a moment of shock, he let out a hoarse, strangled cry and collapsed, waving his hands above his head as if hoping the universe itself might come to his rescue. Heykal jumped, startled by the suddenness of it all. Slowly he approached the man, who lay splayed out on the floor, his fly gaping open; such an enormous mass and so still, as still as a corpse. He was dead. His bulging eyes continued to stare at the governor's portrait with ferocious intensity; to Heykal it looked like the two men were engaged in a grotesque standoff. He left without waiting to discover the reason for this furious antagonism.

The clamor in the casino made Heykal think the news of the stranger's death had already spread, but he soon realized his mistake. Someone had hit the jackpot, and the gamblers were celebrating this outbreak of luck. Heykal took advantage of the sparkling mood to cross the room unnoticed and go out onto the promenade. When he got to the disco, he claimed an empty table next to a dwarf palm and sat down to wait for events to take their course.

There was no doubt the man had suffered a heart attack while looking at the governor's portrait. This death wasn't part of the plan, but Heykal didn't mind—it was the hand of fate (and proof of its sense of humor). The first man to see the poster had dropped dead! As long as the rest don't follow him down this path—in which case we'll be looking at a wholesale slaughter! Heykal didn't want that. Alert to the slightest development, he turned a benevolently ironic gaze on the complacent bourgeoisie gathered there, all pumped up with their pathetic privileges. The casino was the most fashionable spot in the city, with admission restricted to members of the elite. But fascinated though Heykal was by the inanity of the crowd he soon came to a glum realization: these people were all intolerably ugly—an ugliness that was unforgivable, unremitting, and untempered by even a trace of kindness. They weren't even having a good time! They were stuck in their roles, unwitting players in the lugubrious comedy that was unfolding around them. Humanity is ugly: Heykal had always known that. But this—this was almost more than he could bear.

He turned to look at the governor's box, something pleasant to latch onto. There was Soad with her father and the governor. The others had disappeared; even the governor's mistress was gone, probably off to sing in one of the nightclubs. The young girl was seated on the armrest of the governor's chair, and she seemed to be begging him to grant her some favor, using all the charms of her precocious femininity. She leaned toward him and stroked the back of his hand softly, the way people stroke hunchbacks for good luck. The governor, clearly struggling to resist her juvenile attempts at seduction, looked mortified. Heykal couldn't tell what Soad wanted from the governor. It intrigued him, and he continued to watch with curiosity.

The governor was the sort of public figure who stumps even the cleverest caricaturists. What could they do that nature hadn't already accomplished? Short and potbellied, with stubby legs, he had a squashed nose and huge bug eyes ready to pop out of their sockets. Under his gaze, you became a miscreant microbe, magnified a thousand times over by those monstrous, staring orbs. But in fact the governor was only trying to show that in this city of chronic sleepers he was awake. No one could deny that. He saw everything that went on around him; he took himself for an eagle and acted as if he had an eye to match. He'd been appointed governor by one of his army pals (who was promoted to a government minister as a reward for his perfect mediocrity) and jumped at the chance to make up for years of inactivity. He governed the city as if he were commanding a troop of new recruits, inventing prohibitions each day, always with painful consequences for the long-suffering people. You would think he wanted to break a record. The only thing he hadn't dared to outlaw yet was the playing of trictrac in cafés. He was said to be considering it all the time, but so far his advisers had dissuaded him by arguing that trictrac was an essentially reactionary institution that deserved government support.

Soad was standing next to the governor's chair, tugging at his sleeve and gesturing with her head toward the dance floor. At last Heykal understood what she wanted; she wanted the governor to dance with her. But the governor was stubbornly refusing, trying to wrest his arm free while a look of comic alarm spread over his gnomelike face. Heykal felt a flash of admiration for Soad; the girl was going out of her way to put on a great show. At one point, she glanced at him with a malicious smile on her lips, as if to make sure he noticed how much trouble she was taking to provide him with entertainment. It was true: to see the governor dance would be a veritable godsend for anyone with a taste for the local color. Heykal flashed an encouraging smile at Soad, then went back to observing the crowd.

The mood in the room had changed in the last few minutes. There was an imperceptible nervousness among the personnel; the waiters and maître d's were running around looking confused. Several customers had risen hastily and gone into the game room. Around him Heykal could feel the ripples of an underlying tension, a gust of mysterious panic. People who'd been speaking loudly suddenly began to whisper among themselves; others fell silent altogether. Only the orchestra sustained its deafening clamor, but then some mistakes in keeping time made it clear that the musicians, too, were aware that something terrible had happened. Someone, Heykal concluded, must have discovered the dead body on the bathroom floor. His heart fluttered as he thought of what would happen next.

"Hello, Heykal."

Before him was a young man as beautiful as a wild gazelle; his slender face swayed gracefully at the end of a long neck, which set off the extreme prettiness of his delicate features. He had big, bedroom eyes with soft eyelids, and he used them to dazzling effect. He was a particular kind of social climber, a borderline gigolo often seen with women of a certain age and a certain fortune. His name was Riad. One of Riad's ambitions was to get into Heykal's circle, for he admired Heykal without reserve and tried to imitate him whenever he found himself talking to people who were unacquainted with the original. Heykal didn't enjoy his company and kept him at a distance, but Riad's obsessive interest in the goings-on among the city's elite made him valuable; he kept Heykal abreast of the gossip and rumors that were spreading through government circles. Riad flaunted his connections shamelessly; he hoped to dazzle Heykal with the depth of his penetration into the most sophisticated milieu. It never occurred to him that such people disgusted Heykal, that his sole interest in them was as fodder for his cruel humor.

"Heard the news?" Riad said, sitting down at Heykal's table.

"No, but I hope you'll be kind enough to tell me."

Riad paused, batted his eyelashes, and his neck swayed as it always did when he set about charming a reluctant audience. He soon realized that he'd better hurry up. Under the circumstances, he couldn't afford fancy phrases; Heykal might hear the news any minute, and Riad would lose the benefit of bringing it to him. But it pained him to omit the preliminary niceties, so he allowed himself to be just a little mysterious.

"Well, the governor's going to be very happy!"

"Why?" asked Heykal. "Isn't he happy enough already?"

"His worst enemy just died," Riad finally blurted out. "You know, Abdel Halim Makram, the rich industrialist. He had a heart attack in the bathroom of the game room."

"He deserved it," Heykal said. "What an imbecile! How could anyone be the enemy of the governor—such a delightful man!"

"You don't know the story? A few months ago the governor stole his mistress from him—that old relic, Om Khaldoun, the singer. Now she's the governor's trophy."

"But everyone knows Abdel Halim is impotent."

"Doesn't matter. He didn't know everyone knew. On the contrary, he was worried the singer had told the governor—she was a woman, it was inevitable. So he developed a virulent hatred for him. Old men can be terrors when it comes to their virility."

While talking with Riad, Heykal never lost sight of the governor's box. The moment was approaching when the death of Abdel Halim would become common knowledge. He couldn't wait to see how the governor would react. Soad had renounced her magnificent plan to make the governor dance and was sitting quietly next to father, listening with a bored expression as the two men carried on an energetic discussion. The governor looked pained, like someone whose vanity was being bruised; his interlocutor must have been feeding him the usual stream of sarcasm. His mustache twitched and he lifted his hand now and then, as if to fend off the flood of offensive eloquence. Heykal saw Soad yawn with perfect innocence, making a public display of her boredom. In their box, separated from the public, they seemed to be the only ones not affected by the anxiety that was in the air.

"Virility," said Heykal. "Poor Abdel Halim was only so sure he'd lost his because he was wasting it on an old woman with faded charms. His snobbery—his obsessive desire to be the lover of a famous singer—overwhelmed everything else. It would have been unworthy of his fortune to sleep with some unknown young woman who nobody talked about but who would have satisfied his desire. People would call him cheap. He just wanted to impress his fellow citizens."

"That's entirely correct," said Riad. "But that's not all. Would you believe what they found on the wall above the urinal? A poster with a picture of the governor and a text extolling his virtues! Strange coincidence, don't you think?"

"What exactly are you saying? That the portrait of the governor was responsible for the heart attack?"

"Indubitably. Abdel Halim was, by several accounts, drunk. The governor's face looking down on him while he urinated—reminding him, you could say, of their bone of contention...What a terrible shock!"

"Interesting theory," admitted Heykal.

"And it's a crime! You could justifiably claim that the governor killed him. Indirectly, of course, but still—doesn't change the fact that it happened that way. So what do you think of that?"

Once again Riad batted his eyes; he was like a novice hooker who has but a single trick with which to launch her career. He wanted Heykal to know that he too possessed a critical mind, that he could savor the humor of the situation just as much as Heykal. But his plan fell flat. His companion was uninterested.

"Nothing to say?" Riad was downcast. "I would've thought a story like that was made to please you."

"It pleases me enormously," said Heykal, in order not to disappoint the young man totally.

Riad smiled hopefully but without batting his eyes; it was useless. He launched into a violent diatribe against the governor, certain that Heykal would approve.

"The governor has launched a brazen ad campaign," he said. "He must think we're imbeciles. What I read on that poster was absolutely inane—stupefying. His abuse of power has gone too far, don't you think?"

"My dear Riad, you're much too young to be able to appreciate the man and his merits," responded Heykal. "He's an exceptional person; he knows what he's doing. I admire him more and more with each day. Your naiveté pains me."

Riad's delicate, feminine features expressed infinite disappointment, as if he'd just been told of his own death. But it was worse: it was the collapse of a whole way of looking at things he had believed he shared with Heykal. He searched in vain for an appropriate reply to Heykal's condescending allusion to his youth, but his thoughts were interrupted by the distant roar of an ambulance heading toward the casino. It got louder as it approached, piercing the air with its anguished wail. At the sound of this harbinger of disaster, the people around them froze in expectation. Riad, head swaying, looked Heykal up and down, and his smug expression returned, as if the noise of the siren had proved him right. But Heykal had turned back to the governor's box; he was transfixed by the spectacle taking place there. The governor was standing on his chair, scanning the room with his big, bulging eyes in an attempt to locate the origin of the danger; he looked ready to crush a revolution. Then the siren stopped, and Soad let out a peal of laughter. She was looking at Heykal; their eyes met, and his smile was more mocking than ever.

# 9

THAT MORNING, looking out at the sea from high up on his sunny terrace, Karim had had an intuition that the day would be ripe with comical events. Now, giving them time to materialize, he took short, even steps down the long, dusty avenue, stopping from time to time in the shade of one of the bordering trees. He was ready, primed for the unexpected; he noticed the smallest detail of the dizzying spectacle the street presented as workers and people seeking work milled around, ran into him, jostled past, and overwhelmed him with words and gestures that seemed to be invested with an inscrutable, fateful significance. Karim was as happy as could be. Nothing gave him more pleasure than to wander the streets in search of the unexpected. Everything he saw and heard made him indescribably happy, increasing his good cheer. The darkened interiors of the shops looked like dens of mystery, and his mind filled with sensual images of the refinements of seduction, so that he lingered in the doorways hoping to glimpse something thrilling inside. One thing he always hoped to stumble on was the kind of meaningless incident that becomes a pretext for bouts of invective. He loved listening to the men angrily insulting each other in the most colorful language. There was one particular expression that he was always certain to hear every time he observed an altercation between two men. No matter what their social class— and most of the time these fights broke out among the poorest of the poor—one man was sure to say to the other, with an air of outraged dignity, "Don't you know who I am?" This delighted Karim.

How did people come by this exaggerated self-regard? He'd always wanted to find out. It was unbelievable: in this city any old bum took himself for a luminary. Start with the government baptizing that crumbling road by the sea a "strategic route." These delusions of grandeur trickled down from on high! All the arrogant trash-talkers were only following the honorable example of their government.

But it was not just with the intention of taking a leisurely stroll that Karim found himself, at such an early hour, out in the blazing sun on a major thoroughfare and among a sullen mob moving sluggishly through the heat and dust. Yesterday evening he'd received an official summons ordering him to present himself for questioning. This hadn't thrown him in the least; he'd expected it. It was the follow-up to the inquiry the police were conducting because of the cursed strategic route. So well before the appointed hour he'd gone out to savor the atmosphere of the street at leisure and to prepare himself for the interrogation, which would determine whether he could stay on in his new apartment. While he dawdled, he wondered if that old wheezy policeman who'd risked death to climb up his six flights of stairs a week earlier had kept his promise to write a favorable report. Would he, after accepting the kite, turn out to be an ingrate? Karim replayed the scene in his memory—the painful hesitation of the aging father who suspected a bribe. That he might have succeeded in corrupting an officer in the line of duty made him laugh, but only for an instant; he didn't feel calm at all. He'd still have to answer pointless questions and grovel and snivel in order to get them to forgive his past as a revolutionary. It required preparation. Like an actor getting ready for the role of his life, he began to transform himself into the picture of humility, twisting his face into the expression of someone crushed by the burden of his responsibilities. Unfortunately there was no mirror, no window in which to examine himself. To rehearse a role of such import without being able to correct the inevitable flaws—and however small, they could still cause damage—was proving an arduous, challenging task. He tried resuming his normal look, smiling broadly to erase the expression of suffering from his face. No matter what, he was sure to disgust them, all those idiot cops who wanted to kick him out of his comfortable lodging and throw him into a hovel in the slums. He was attached to his spacious terrace and the sea breeze, both essential for testing his kites. But more than that, it was a question of honor—above all because of that ineffably ingenuous "strategic route." It was really too beautiful; how could he not plumb it to its most ludicrous depths? He just had to make sure to stick to his plan, acting inoffensive and obsequious, almost simpleminded, careful never to utter an intelligent word—that was the biggest risk. To demonstrate intelligence was as good as spitting in their faces. But how was he going to dim the sardonic glint in his eyes? Dark glasses? Pretend he had conjunctivitis? What a marvelous idea! Why hadn't he thought of it earlier? But it was too late now, and anyway, he couldn't afford to buy the glasses.

From time to time, his eyes fell on one of the posters he'd put up the night before in anticipation of today's walk. Strewing his path with pictures of the governor had seemed brilliant then, when he'd been filled with the delighted anticipation of today's walk, but now he regretted having anything to do with this hideous thing that accosted him with every step, like a billboard from hell. The posters made him sick; it was all too depressing. Already a few of them had fallen victim to local vandals, with eyes scratched out or a beard scribbled in. These perfidious flourishes hadn't ruined the governor completely; he was still recognizable. Since the appearance of the posters, he'd become as famous as a movie star. Even children cursed him, like the villain of an action film. But that didn't bother the authorities in the least; what bothered them was when crowds gathered around to look and laugh, peppering their laughter with jibes and snide asides. More than once the police had to intervene, arresting a few individuals who were laughing especially loudly, charging them with public drunkenness. Which was, come to think of it, more or less true. And then there were always two or three hash smokers around, and for them the governor's picture triggered explosions of transcendent glee. Nothing could temper their hysterical outbursts—not even the billy clubs of the policemen, who were furious to see the effects of drug use spreading to contaminate the lives of clean-living citizens, who no doubt were stunned by such unmerited praise of the governor but still maintained appearances as best they could. These bouts of collective hilarity—which would spring up at the most inopportune moments, sometimes causing traffic jams—were putting the authorities to the test. The government's henchmen waited dejectedly, utterly confounded by the treacherous initiative, which seemed unworthy of real revolutionaries and bordered on being a hoax.

Karim stopped abruptly. A few meters ahead, under the shade of one of the trees lining the avenue, a traveling barber had set up with his tools. Karim wondered if he should get his hair cut. Suddenly it seemed vital that he appear well-groomed when presenting himself to the authorities, so that they would recognize the esteem in which he held them. A haircut was essential: long hair suggested the tortured spirit of a bitter revolutionary. And his scruffy neck and sideburns—not respectable. What a serious mistake he'd almost made! How would they know he'd reformed when he had a mop on his head befitting a dirty intellectual? A good haircut—an almost shaved head, like a convict's—that would make the right impression! That would be concrete proof of his loyalty! And only one man could perform this miracle: this ignorant barber, with his clippers of mass destruction.

Karim sauntered up, delighted with his decision.

The barber was in the midst of shaving an earnest young man wearing a dark, tattered suit, with a morose expression and an air of dignified poverty. He sat on a wooden stool with his back pressed against a tree and his eyes closed, and the impression he made was one of exquisite agony. On his knees was a paper folder on which he had laid his threadbare tarboosh, the distinctive sign of a public servant—he looked like he was afraid of being dragged into the surrounding human scum. The barber squatted and, with the meticulous gestures of an embalmer preparing a corpse, shaved his customer's cheeks with a razor so old and broken that it rasped like a power saw. Karim's arrival didn't disturb them at all; neither of them answered his greeting. Surprised, but as confident as ever of his plan, he sank down on the second stool the barber provided for waiting clients. Right away he felt a subtle change in the atmosphere, filling him with an incredible happiness, irresistibly nudging him little by little toward sleep. The cool shade and the scent of the shaving soap mingled with the violet perfume of various oils and tonics were like the sweet air of the countryside. It was hot as a furnace, but the barber's spot—though still outdoors—was a garden of delights, a place to draw you into dreams. Karim would have liked to stay as long as possible, motionless, only half-conscious as people swirled about, writhing like the damned in the eternal fire. He was still savoring this exquisite respite when he was brutally torn from his torpor by a donkey cart coming to a screeching halt at the curb. The driver leaped to the ground, unhitched his donkey, and, grabbing it by the neck, hauled it into the shade practically right under Karim's nose.

"Master Abadou," the driver croaked, "are you going to be done soon? This son of a bitch needs grooming!"

"Right away," the barber responded, tossing a glance at the four-legged client. "Just a minute, and I'll take care of him."

The donkey, either out of vanity or because he understood that they were talking about him, started to bray without interruption, which Karim found very disagreeable. After a moment of this, the young man couldn't restrain himself from addressing the driver:

"Does it bray like that all the time, or is it his birthday?"

"He's hot," said the driver. "He's an old donkey, but a good one."

The driver was a fat brute, incapable of appreciating sarcasm. Karim was deeply pained; he'd hoped for a wittier reply. Faced with his interlocutor's intellectual paucity he looked put out, saying:

"I'm sure he is. But try anyway to make him shut up. It's unbearable!"

The driver patted the donkey on the back, soothing it like a mistress with tender words, promising it unheard-of heaps of alfalfa. In response to these false vows, the donkey gradually calmed down and began to chew at the air. By this time the barber had finished with his client, who donned his tarboosh and slipped away, folder under his arm, aware that an altercation was brewing. Clearly he didn't want to be implicated in a fight over a donkey.

Master Abadou grabbed his clippers and approached the donkey with the nervous look of an artist finally taking on his great subject. But before he could get to work, Karim stopped him with a gesture and stood up from his stool.

"What's this, man! I was here first. And I'm in a hurry!"

"Excuse me, effendi," said the driver. "But he's a regular, I can't make him wait."

"He'll wait. I'm telling you: I'm in a hurry."

"This donkey is in a bigger hurry than you, young man," said the driver.

"Why?" said Karim. "Is he going to a wedding?"

"We don't have time for weddings," came the driver's grandiloquent reply. "We work!"

The donkey started braying again, as if proud of the prerogative he enjoyed. Singing sweetly to nobody, the barber ran the clippers along his back. Karim, though only feigning indignation, was increasingly exercised by the care that was being lavished on the donkey. What was this beast? A government donkey—a minister, perhaps, traveling incognito to gain insight into his subjects' state of mind? That wouldn't be at all surprising, given the exceptional treatment he was enjoying at the barber's hands. What a crazy situation! Karim had gotten trapped in a maze and he'd have to find a clever way out that wasn't going to cause too much damage. But he couldn't leave, just like that, without making some kind of scene—abandoning such a fertile terrain just waiting for the seeds of conflict to be sown. This could be his only chance all day to have some fun.

He lifted his cuff, pretending to check the watch on his wrist, and addressed the barber once more:

"Do you realize, man, I have a meeting with the governor. And you're making me wait behind a donkey!"

"Which governor?" said the driver, as if frankly stunned to learn of the existence of such a person.

"What do you mean, which governor?" exploded Karim. "The governor of this city!"

"This city is governed?" said the driver. "Don't tell me that, young man; I won't believe you."

"No wonder things are falling to pieces!" cried Karim. "You and your kind are turning us into a bunch of savages!"

The craziness had reached its peak, but Karim wasn't capable of stopping the mechanism he'd set off. A familiar demon goaded him to push things even further, to see just how far this absurd conversation could be taken. On top of that, he was reluctant to leave the cool shade and launch out into the torrid atmosphere of the avenue and the hassle of a police interrogation.

"I'm leaving," he said with conviction. But he didn't leave. He was waiting for something—as if expecting some dazzling beam of light revealing the secrets of humanity to emerge from the situation.

"Wait, effendi," said the barber, as he clipped big tufts of fur from the donkey. "I'll be finished soon. It'll be your turn in a minute."

"I will not follow a donkey," responded Karim proudly. "You don't seem to have any idea whom you're speaking to!"

The barber thought for a moment, clippers in suspense, his features twisted in apprehension. Intrigued, he asked:

"Well, who are you, effendi?"

"I'm not going to waste my time telling you," Karim flippantly responded. "Go on and take care of that donkey—that's your kind of customer!"

"Did I just hear you insulting my donkey?" cried the driver, wild-eyed. "Who do you think you are to insult someone who works for a living?"

The word was out: a worker! So as far as this pathetic bunch was concerned, the donkey had the right to be respected, not as an animal but for its noble status as a worker. For a few seconds, Karim was blinded by the sheer deliciousness of this—a recompense at last for his long wait. He turned his back on the two men and hurled himself deliberately into the furnace: all was well with the world.

He had to resist further experimentation. After the scene at the barber's he was running late, and he'd have to hurry to get to city hall at the appointed hour. He felt cheerful, full of optimism—in good enough shape, in any case, to confront the sadistic, power-hungry officers who would be assigned to his interrogation. Moved by this feeling of joy, he broke into a trot, making his way with difficulty through the careless crowd clogging the avenue.

He stopped, out of breath, to examine the big white building topped by a flag—city hall and the seat of the governor. It was a long time since he'd been here. He hesitated before crossing the threshold, remembering his brash attitude on previous visits, when he'd been a reckless and arrogant revolutionary. He felt ashamed recalling his former foolishness. How could he have failed to understand that they were stronger than he was, that all his bluster only played into their hands, hurting his cause by putting him on the same level as his enemies? Happily, things had taken a new turn since that far-off time; he would shock them silly. He lowered his head and tried to look humble and timid, then entered through the monumental double doors, which opened wide like a trap ready to snap up its prey. He shivered, and a cold sweat ran down his back—it was not fear but the effect of suddenly coming into the cool air of the great building. He tried to shrink away even more, camouflaging himself as a citizen without ideas or ambitions, a creature who submitted to fate and trembled before every kind of authority. In this character he was no different from the other people who filled the vast room on the ground floor, coming and going like figures in a nightmare, eyes fixedly staring as they shuttled from one office to another, delivered into the caprice of the vindictive machine. Karim acted like someone who was familiar with the place; without bothering to ask directions he headed straight to the flight of wide stone stairs and climbed to the second floor. An orderly, seated behind a table, was reading his newspaper without moving a muscle on his face; probably he couldn't read and was only pretending. Karim handed him his summons. The man took it, gave it a sideways glance, and murmured:

"Follow me."

Karim followed him silently, staying in character as a poor, harmless wretch. The orderly opened a door, let Karim in, and closed it behind him softly, as if to avoid waking a sleeper. Karim noticed the typical smell of an interrogation room: an undefinable scent, mental more than olfactory, as if human absurdity emitted a nauseating stench. People of all types and from all over waited on benches along the walls, their expressions frozen with resignation so excessive that it looked put on. They seemed to have been there forever, covered in dust, their clothes all worn out; they were like sculptures from another era that had just been dug up. Karim gazed at them briefly, stupefied, like someone viewing a catacomb and its relics for the first time. He pulled his handkerchief from his pocket and mopped the sweat off his forehead to prove to himself that he was still alive, but already he knew the sinister truth: all these people were playing the same game he was. If they were mute and looked lifeless, it was in the hopeless hope that they would be taken for dead. This, of all possible attitudes, was the one that was least exposed to tyranny's talons. Karim admired their act of dissimulation and, only too happy to get a close-up look at these models of humanity, found an open spot on one of the benches and sat down, mimicking their pitiful posture. For a moment he stayed there, neutrally still, playing dead in this disparate gathering of mute victims; then, with an abundance of circumspection, he risked a glance toward the back of the room. Seated behind his desk, a uniformed security officer was exhaustively interrogating a bleary-eyed man with the look of a piecemeal skeleton, apparently a spy from some miserable desert country. Just behind them, two police-men with military mustaches stood at attention. Karim recognized the officer: it was Hatim, the one who'd taken care of him back in the day. This discovery surprised and irked him at the same time; he thought the new regime would have had the good sense to change their policemen. How naive! And yet he should have known: the simple truth, enduring and unchallenged, was that the power of the police outlasted every regime.

From the back of the room he heard Hatim's voice, scathing and angry; the officer seemed to be having some serious problems with an informant. Karim heard the latter let out a long sigh in response to his torturer's repeated interrogations, as if advanced tuberculosis prevented him from articulating a single word. Hatim made a strange face in front of this mute, emaciated stool pigeon. To keep from bursting into laughter, Karim had to remember his own situa-tion—it was far from stellar. He was going to have to revise all his plans. How could he play his game with Hatim, who knew all about him? Hatim wouldn't walk right into his trap. Karim's moral and physical transformation—even after all these years—would make him highly suspicious. Perhaps he should refine his act, introduce a modicum of dignity, the kind of dignity that Hatim, in his barbaric cruelty, would relish breaking. Karim decided to offer him this pal-try gift as a sign of his esteem.

Hatim suddenly seemed to have had enough of his stool pigeon; with a furious gesture he turned him over to one of the guards. For a moment he appeared to relax and breathe more easily, as if set free;

then he started scrutinizing the people seated on the benches. He seemed to be looking for somebody specific and kept shaking his head with a disappointed frown. Suddenly a spark lit up in his eyes; he'd just recognized Karim in this heap of human garbage. His nostrils flared, a thin smile fluttered on his lips, and he seemed to bloom with renewed vigor and aggression.

"Karim effendi!" he yelled, pointing to the young man.

Karim rose and went to stand in front of the police officer.

"Hello, Your Excellency!" he said in his humblest voice, his eyes lowered, and in a posture of uttermost contrition.

The officer looked taken aback; he stared closely at Karim as if perhaps he'd mistaken his identity.

"I must be dreaming!" he said. "You never acted like this before. What's happened to you?"

Karim kept his eyes down and said nothing. He was aware that the entire interrogation would depend on his reply. He was searching for the right words when Hatim resumed:

"Sit down. You have no idea how happy I am to see you."

Karim sat on the chair that the stool pigeon had just vacated and looked up at the officer with an expression of unquestionable sincerity.

"I know I was wrong, Your Excellency! Can't the police simply forget about me?"

"Forget you!" exclaimed Hatim. "But you left such unforgettable memories! You wanted to destroy everything. You promised to have me hung once you and your friends were in power. Those were your very words, or am I mistaken?"

"That was foolishness," said Karim. "I was joking, Your Excellency! How could you have thought that I was serious?"

"What are you talking about? Do you take me for an imbecile?"

"No, God help me, Your Excellency! In a moment of madness I might have said such things. And things were different then. You forget, Your Excellency, that was during the old regime."

"And? Are you a revolutionary, yes or no? Can you explain to me in what way the new regime is more satisfactory than all the others?"

"It's hard to explain," admitted Karim, crestfallen. "But you can feel it, there's no doubt. With a good regime, even the air is different. For example, just now, walking in the street, it seemed to me that it was not so hot as it used to be."

"Ah! It's not so hot now! That's the sole benefit you find in the new regime?"

"I am sure the new regime has brought other benefits, but perhaps I'm not aware of them, Your Excellency."

Now this was talking! Karim was almost proud of himself for coming up with that one. But the officer looked worried; the young man's display of humility had thrown him off. Could he be joking? Unlikely. He knew Karim's mentality very well; nothing about it indicated he'd go in for such trifles. Then what? It was a mystery, and for now he was stumped, but he meant to clear it up before going any further.

Hatim had expected to do battle with a stubborn adversary, and he found himself facing a human worm. Notwithstanding his professional duties, he'd found occasion at every turn to admire the courage—the indomitable revolutionary spirit—that had driven the young man. And he'd been happy at the prospect of measuring himself against him once more. He'd learned a lot from these revolutionaries, things that had been very good for his career. Among higher-ups, Hatim was known for having studied the subject of subversion from every angle; he was considered a highly sophisticated officer, capable of combating the twisted theories of all the young madmen who wanted to overthrow the powers that be. In fact, his whole knowledge of such matters consisted of snippets torn out of political prisoners in the course of interrogation. So he resented Karim's grotesque attitude. This son of a bitch wasn't giving him anything positive to display in front of his superiors. Not as hot as it was under other regimes? He was making fun of him, for sure.

Anger boiled up inside Hatim, but he contained it. He examined the young man with the concern of a psychiatrist trying to detect a glimmer of dawning sanity in a patient. But Karim refused to react. He stayed in character: humble, tragically pitiable. Hatim's eyes widened; he was thoroughly disappointed. He viewed the prospect of accepting the young man's repentance with genuine displeasure. And he still didn't quite believe it—it was just too easy. Revolutionaries don't change, at least not like this. Like cops, they were indifferent to regimes.

He sighed deliberately to show that he wasn't giving up yet. Then he opened the file in front of him and leafed through it with a shrewd, penetrating eye. As he read, his face became more pensive, more preoccupied, as if this hunt for a clue that would put the interrogation back on course had taken on some more dramatic importance. Suddenly he raised his head and stared at the young man, a passionate gleam in his eyes. He seemed to be on the track of a particularly serious offense. Karim pretended to shiver a little with fear, allowing himself the luxury of spoiling his adversary.

"According to the report of the agent who visited you, it appears that you are working. You make kites. Is that right?"

"It's hard to make a living, Your Excellency. I do what I can."

"Well then, tell me a bit about these kites. What do they look like?"

Hatim's suspicious look—on top of this stupid question—was the height of bad melodrama. Karim hadn't predicted this. Did the officer imagine he used the kites to photograph military targets? Why not? Anything's possible in the realm of police fantasy.

"They're small kites, Your Excellency. Completely humble. What did you think they were?"

"Don't worry about what I think. But tell me what they're for."

"For entertaining children, nothing more."


Hatim didn't seem convinced, and Karim was choking painfully from holding back an enormous outburst of laughter. The officer continued to stare suspiciously; he didn't believe the simple story. These kites had to have some secret purpose, but the terrain was tricky and he hesitated to go too far; there might be traps, and he risked losing ground. He moved his hand as if to swat a fly; it was how he dealt with thorny cases.

"Let's forget about that for now," he said. "And tell me what you think of the situation in general. Speak frankly."

"I think that everything is going well, Your Excellency. Really, I don't see anything going badly. My impression is that the people are content; they're the picture of perfect happiness."

"Well, let me inform you that you're too optimistic. There are still plenty of bastards out there, bitter people who continue to complain. It seems they're not content with the new regime, either. What do we have to do to make them happy, I ask you?"

"I don't know, Your Excellency. I don't bother with politics anymore. I'm about to get married."

These last words had a catastrophic effect on Hatim.

"You're going to get married?" he asked, his face twisted in disgust.

"Yes, Your Excellency," responded Karim, in the voice of a man who was about to commit suicide.

Hatim snapped his file shut; he seemed to banish the young man from his universe. Already his gaze was distant as he said:

"Well, for the moment you may stay where you are. But watch out: the slightest prank and I'll make you vacate your apartment."

Karim was about to thank him when a door opened and the governor himself appeared. Hatim rose, followed by Karim and the whole ensemble of characters who'd been prostrate on the benches. For a few seconds, the governor remained on the threshold of his office, surveying the room with bulging eyes; then he began to walk, trotting on bent legs as if riding a horse. He was just passing by, when Karim—as if moved by a sudden impulse—intercepted him, seizing his hand and kissing it while murmuring a few

unintelligible words. Karim returned to his place, panting shamelessly with excitement, as if crushed by the weight of an undeserved
blessing. The governor wasn't the least bit offended nor did he break
his pace; he was accustomed to such signs of veneration. Superb on
his invisible horse, he trotted on, until at last he left the room.

Karim's unsettling act had left Hatim totally distraught. Expecting
an attack, he'd tried to stop it, but what he'd seen instead was far
worse: it was the world turned upside down. This Karim, whom he
thought he knew so well, had suddenly become incomprehensible
to him. He stared with horrified eyes, as if at a monster. Karim, for
his part, was in seventh heaven. He'd risked everything for this
simple pleasure: leaving Hatim thunderstruck, with irrefutable
proof of his repentance. And there was no doubt he'd succeeded in
this exploit.

Hatim signaled for Karim to sit back down.
    "By God!" said Hatim. "You surprise me more and more."
    "Why, Your Excellency?"
    "It's hard for me to believe that you would come to this: kissing
the governor's hand!"
    "That's not in the least surprising," said Karim. "The governor is
our father, a father to all of us; at least, that's how I see it."

Hatim thought for a second. His interest in the young man intensi-
fied. In the horrifying light of the immeasurable degradation here
spread before his eyes, he began to see an escape from the private
calvary of dutiful public servant. Maybe all was not yet lost.
    "So since that's the way it is, maybe we can collaborate. You
wouldn't like it, would you, if your father—as you put it—were the
object of vicious attacks?"
    "Of course not. But what can I do?"

"I'd like to know your opinion of certain posters that have recently appeared on the walls of the city."

"What posters?" Karim asked innocently.

"Allow me to enlighten you," said Hatim. "These posters feature the governor's portrait and praise him in glorious terms, too glorious to be sincere. Have you seen them?"

"Those posters, Your Excellency? Those are beautiful posters! Every time I see one, I stop to read it. I've learned the text by heart, in fact. Would you like me to recite it?"

"Save yourself the trouble. Instead can you tell me who's behind them? Who's printing them? Who's putting them up on walls all over the city?"

"But, Your Excellency, I assumed it was the government. The posters say nothing but good about our kind governor!"

"You're mistaken. The government didn't print these posters! Don't you think it's your old comrades who made them?"

"What a thought!" exclaimed Karim. "I don't know what to say! Why would my old comrades sing the praises of the governor?"

"Maybe they've gone mad. I'm trying to understand."

He was extremely unhappy to reveal to Karim the awkward position the posters had put him in. But the slightest clue could mean an unhoped-for release; if he tracked down the creators of this poisonous panegyric that had the entire police force on alert, his reputation as an astute officer would be beyond all suspicion. In twenty years of working with political offenses he'd never seen anything like this—a problem so serious, and at the same time so delicate, so out of the ordinary, that there was no mention of it in any of the police manuals. Hatim wondered if this wasn't the beginning of a new revolutionary era—he might have to revise his investigatory technique. A new way of doing things had been born, and there he sat like an idiot, unaware of the birthplace or the identity of the instigators. He was overcome by panic.

"So you know nothing?"

It wasn't a question so much as a last attempt to seize a bit of the truth. He waited for Karim's reply without much hope.

"Nothing, Your Excellency," Karim responded glumly. He gazed at Hatim with an empty, defeated expression.

A painful feeling of failure took hold of Hatim, darkening his already formidable features. The interrogation was ending in weakness and defeat. He had extracted nothing from this repentant revolutionary on his way to the altar, who made kites for the amusement of a bunch of brats. Was it possible to sink lower? He was surprised to feel a sort of regret—in this case particularly absurd. Could he really feel pity for a failed revolutionary? There were plenty of others, all sorts of people seeking revenge, happy to sow the seeds of disorder along the way. And yet something had died: a tiny spark in the raging fire that wanted to set the world ablaze.

He leaned his elbows on his desk, covered his forehead with his hands, and said, without looking at Karim:

"You may leave now."

Karim got up, made a low bow, turned on his heel, and fled. As he left, he nodded right and left to his unhappy successors. But they paid no attention. Quietly closing the door behind him, as he'd seen the orderly do, he left the room.

A little ways down the avenue, which was now nearly deserted, he stopped in the shade of a tree and turned back to survey the distance he'd traversed from city hall. The big white building had vanished like a mirage behind the haze of heat. Karim felt like he was emerging from a dream.

# IO

KARIM was relaxing. He leaned against the stone parapet that ran along the cliff road and studied the languid asses of the women strolling by, so plainly visible beneath their light dresses. How different they all were! They came in every shape and size. In the veiled gray light of dusk, these amazing asses took on a life of their own, promising him sensuous delights. The owners of the asses were, for the most part, so ugly that even a sex maniac would run screaming, but Karim barely noticed; he seldom looked at a woman's face. Most of the women were accompanied by plain fat men dressed for the summer heat, men who wore striped cotton pajama pants and had their shirtsleeves rolled up as they munched on watermelon seeds while watching over their wives and daughters and keeping an eye on Karim, glaring at him like a peasant guarding his cows from a cattle thief. It made Karim snicker to see their sullen distrust. Every evening it was the same: families out on a ritual stroll looking for cool air, eager to breathe the sea breeze after the stifling heat of the day. And for Karim this procession of wistful asses was his daily break; he would come down from his terrace to lean against the parapet and wait for opportunity to strike. From time to time he'd be lucky enough to find a woman out on her own, looking for adventure, and he'd accost her in a direct and primitive way. Karim was as unforthcoming with women as he was with the police. He never said an intelligent word for fear of scaring them off; one dumb remark about the weather and the deal was done.

But tonight, nothing; prey was scarce. During the hour he'd been there, he hadn't seen a single potential victim. All the women who went by were accompanied, or else they were bitter nannies dragging little kids in their wake. Karim was getting annoyed. A pair of lovers, fingers entwined as if for dear life, passed in front of him with an expression of affected ecstasy. Karim mechanically followed the young woman's ass with his eyes and was stabbed by a sudden memory—not just a memory of conquest, because he vaguely remembered the girl's face: that sweet little prostitute he'd picked up one night and never seen again, even though he'd invited her to consider his apartment her home. He'd conducted himself with munificence! True, at this moment he didn't really want to see her again; the invitation had been tossed out at a critical moment in order to mollify her and to invite some discretion when it came to the money business. Perhaps she hadn't been fooled and had understood that he didn't have any. A wave of pity swept over him and—how extraordinary!—the face of the little prostitute took shape in his mind, like a face he'd always known, as familiar as the face of his own mother. Suddenly he regretted having been so stingy with the poor girl. Where was she now? He wanted to go look for her. The police must have picked her up and scared her off the street. Another victim of the accursed governor.

Speaking of which, it had been two weeks now since Heykal's letter—he'd called for the public to fund the erection of a statue of the governor—had been published in the papers. This letter had created consternation even among those who were most attached to the governor and his dictatorial ways. Already rumors were circulating that the central government did not look favorably on this popularity; doubts had arisen about a man capable of organizing such a successful propaganda campaign on his own behalf. Still, unwitting citizens—unaware of the direction things were heading—had been inspired to demonstrate their civic duty. Money had flowed from everywhere—like manna from heaven that nothing could prevent from falling. The list of donors grew longer with each morning's paper. Karim himself wanted to take part and spent his last penny to support the statue, though his name hadn't been mentioned. Now he bitterly regretted the donation, especially since his meager offering had received such a paltry response. Some readers—whether out of cynicism or naiveté—had written in to the journals to recommend a sculptor of their acquaintance or to indicate a preference as to the future placement of the statue. The craziness had now come to a head, and Heykal was only waiting to execute a new prank if this last one wasn't sufficient to permanently discredit the governor. Karim was meeting with him this evening to discuss the whole question. The position of the governor had been dealt a solid blow, but unforeseen developments had to be kept in mind. Deep down, Karim hoped the governor would hang on for another month or two, long enough to be immortalized in a statue. How funny if things came to that—to see the governor on a pedestal! With only a little luck, it just might happen.

Night had fallen slowly and all at once the streetlamps came on above the cliff road, stretched like a string of gleaming pearls. But even though the air had become more breathable, cooler temperatures hadn't arrived. The smell of grilled corn on the cob, emanating from the cart of a street vendor, filled the night. The road was gradually emptied of its strolling families; only the odd couple straggled by, retreating into shadowy corners to enjoy a quick, shameful spasm.

Karim, despairing of ever finding a girl, was about to leave when his eyes fell on the profile of a man leaning over the parapet at some distance to his left. The man turned quickly as if to hide his face from view. He was standing outside the pool of light made by the nearest streetlamp, but Karim, shocked, had recognized the furtive attitude and conspiratorial pose. The solitary man hiding in the shadows was Taher, his old friend from the revolutionary party; it had been a long time since he'd seen him, but he was certain he wasn't mistaken. He'd identified him at a single glance; for Karim, Taher would be recognizable in the darkest of nights. His heart began to beat with emotion. He felt faint, moved by this miraculous, unexpected encounter with his old friend, but almost immediately a terrible suspicion seized him. The encounter was far from fortuitous; Taher must have been spying on him for a good while already. What for? Why didn't he just come up and say hello? But to ask such questions was to not know Taher. He was a born conspirator, who loved detours and long, secret pursuits; he would never approach somebody without indulging in some mysterious behavior first. Karim decided to let him play his bizarre game. He had some time to kill before going to Heykal's anyway.

He began to walk slowly, giving Taher the chance to spy on him at leisure. It tore at his heart to find himself in Taher's company again; he had no desire to discuss social and political problems with him: their estrangement was permanent. And Taher must resent him for his defection—he might treat him harshly. Still, he couldn't help but recall old memories. He and Taher had spent every minute plotting subversive actions; they were arrested together and taken to the same prison. He was the friend who had been closest to him in spirit, loved and admired for his noble sense of justice and his courage in the face of adversity. He was a smart boy from a family of poor workers who'd forgone food to give him an education. After successfully finishing school he'd refused to take a respectable job, devoting himself entirely to the revolution. His hatred of the powerful was nonnegotiable.

Suddenly Karim recalled a visual detail—something he'd noticed and forgotten. He'd seen that Taher was carrying a package under his arm, and now it came to him that his friend had had a habit of walking with a homemade bomb. Whenever someone asked him what he was planning to do with it, he'd snarl: "There's no shortage of bastards—I'll find somewhere to throw it!" Karim felt certain that Taher hadn't abandoned his strange ways—the package he was carrying had to be a bomb—and he was scared now that he might be attacked. Taher was fully capable of throwing a bomb in his face without a shred of pity, even more so because he considered him a traitor. Karim knew his mentality and his revolutionary code of honor. Taher wouldn't hesitate to throw a bomb at his own mother if she happened not to share his opinion about something. With growing unease, Karim looked for a way to escape his pursuer. Anxiously he inspected the long deserted road without finding a single dark corner to hide in. Just the corn-vendor's cart on the sidewalk lit by the streetlamp. Hide behind the cart? Idiotic. It would roll away without him—the merchant was getting ready to close up shop, as if he'd had a premonition of impending disaster. Karim picked up his pace, feeling vaguely ridiculous and not daring to turn around to see if Taher was still following him. A coarse voice addressed him, stopping him dead.

"Hey, Karim! You don't have to run away from me!"

Karim turned around, a forced smile on his lips. He was as nervous as a woman seeing an old lover she's betrayed and abandoned. He opened his arms in a sign of welcome.

"Hello, Taher, my brother! What a happy coincidence. How are you?"

He wanted to embrace Taher, but his former friend flinched and made a point of pulling back.

"I'm doing very well," replied Taher. "And you? Still having fun?"

"Yes, I'm all right. Believe me, I'm happy to see you. It's been a long time since I've laid eyes on you."

"I'm sorry," said Taher, "but I was in prison. It was hard for me to make it out to the salons and cafés."


Taher's face, gaunt and creased from hardship and a lifetime of trouble, made his outcast state all too clear. His eyes glinted with a wild intransigence common to those who fight for a hopeless cause. He scrutinized Karim suspiciously but with a sense of suppressed tenderness, too, a feeling of sympathy for his comrade—a traitor to the cause, but someone who was still present in his memory. Basically he was as nervous as Karim, even though he was playing the roles of accuser and pitiless judge. His clothes were preposterous for a man in his straits. In every season, he wore a tight brown suit in quite decent condition, a shirt with a starched collar, and a dark tie—the austere outfit of a low-level office worker and a striking contrast to his starving revolutionary's face; he was like two characters superimposed on each other. But that was Taher's great principle: a real revolutionary must dress correctly! The bohemian attitude of some of his comrades made him beside himself with anger; he'd often attacked Karim for not wearing a tie.

Karim was at a loss for words at his friend's news. Prison couldn't have been fun for Taher, who took everything so hard. Karim felt a flash of guilt for standing there, the picture of health and happiness, in front of this man who had escaped from the deepest dungeons in order to accuse him and curse him. Despite himself, he couldn't stop eyeing the package that Taher still held in his hand. He was ashamed of his fear, but it was stronger than he was; he trembled, thinking of the bomb. Taher noticed his nervousness with a withering sigh. Finally something had amused him.

"Don't worry about the package," he said sarcastically. "It's not a bomb. These are my old shoes that I'm taking to the cobbler. The soles have completely come off. You can see: I'm walking barefoot at the moment."

"How could you think...!" Karim protested feebly.

Still, he lowered his eyes to be sure that Taher was telling the truth: in fact, his friend's feet were bare. For an instant he was transfixed, unable to look away from Taher's feet. To wear a starched collar and no shoes, how strange! Karim didn't know whether to laugh or cry.

"I'm truly sorry, brother!"

"Don't be; it's not at all important. I've endured every possible misery. I don't need to live in an apartment with a terrace. I love palaces—I love to destroy them!"

"It's a servant's quarters!" Karim exclaimed. Then, more quietly: "How do you know where I live? You've been spying on me!"

Taher smiled mockingly, as if Karim was a naive child who needed everything explained.

"We know everything about you," he said. "You think you're so clever, but we know everything you're up to, you and your friends. Did you know that the police suspect us for your nonsense? We won't tolerate it much longer. That's why I want to speak to you."

Without thinking, he adopted a conspiratorial voice—inexplicably, since the road was devoid of a single human soul.

"What nonsense?" asked Karim, irritated by his hissing.

"The posters sucking up to the governor—you think I don't know where they come from?"

"What is it about them that bothers you?"

"They make us look ridiculous to the police. And I don't like that. We're not pranksters!"

Taher was outraged at the thought that the police took him for a clown for using such primitive means to overturn the government. To impute these types of inanities to him was to attack his honor as a revolutionary. It besmirched his entire past as a militant, all his years in prison. He saw himself sinking in the esteem of the police, and he fumed with rage. And at the same time his pain was tinged with sorrow because it was his old comrade in arms, this traitor turned puppet, who was responsible for the affront.

"Don't worry about that," said Karim. "The police don't suspect you one bit. They know perfectly well that you're a serious bunch." He added, as if for his own sake: "Just like them. Let me tell you something. You're out of the loop. The police aren't ignorant of the fact that your brand of revolutionary would never do something like this. Don't you know they're making progress all the time? Thanks first of all to what your people leaked during interrogations, but also to the fact that the government has given manuals to the secret police, in which they explain your psychology and how to combat your theories. So you see, they know all about you now. They know that you could never change your ways so drastically."

"In any case, *you*'ve changed," Taher responded bitterly.

By mutual agreement, they'd sat down on the parapet, facing the sea. They were quiet, their gazes lost in the immense black void. Karim was savoring this moment of reconciliation. But Taher's mania, his need to win or die, could know no peace. Slowly he turned toward Karim, awaiting a gesture, a word of repentance or regret. He felt the sadness of a terrorist pressed into action, having to go about his bloody work despite the love and tenderness that still drew him to his victim. His heart bled, and he wanted to beg Karim to renounce this foolishness, to resume the idealism of his past. Sweat drowned his shrunken features; he might as well have been covered in tears.

Taher's look pierced Karim like a dart. His heart bled, too. He was angry at his old friend for having reappeared to remind him of those dark times, which stank of pain and suffering. He had made his peace with this laughable, detestable world. He didn't want to change anything; he took it for what it was, and its blind and lame inhabitants with it. It was like a giant gesture of love. He no longer believed in the impoverishment of the people. Was he rich? He was the poorest of the poor, and yet happy for it. Suddenly his feelings rebelled against this scowling ghost that had come from the past to rip away his joy, and in a provocative, proud voice he said:

"Yes, I've changed. And I'm glad of it."

Taher leaped upon him. He grabbed him by the back of his jacket and held him against the parapet.

"Do you know that our comrades are imprisoned and tortured, while you're out happily postering the walls of the city with praise for their executioner?"

"Listen, Taher! It's not like I slept with your sister! What I did do, you'll never get. But it's the only way to fight the governor, believe me."

"A funny way!" snickered Taher. "I know your master, you know. I've heard all about him. He's the governor's sort: a landlord who lives like a prince. What can he know about the pain of the people?"

"Leave him alone!" Karim shouted. "I love that man, understand! Believe me, not only will I never leave him, but if he asked me to, I'd die for him!"

Taher felt his blood drain away. The violence of Karim's passion suffocated him; it was blasphemy. For him it was only possible to love the people. And because Karim was part of the people, he'd never completely lost his feelings of affection and confidence. He'd pardoned Karim's turpitude, always hoping that their separation was only temporary, that Karim would be faithfully driven to the revolution once again. But now he saw how far his comrade had strayed —from him, from the idea for which he'd fought and suffered. Taher saw that he was acting in an entirely new universe, in which he was not only excluded but was an object of mockery. Jealousy pierced him, opening a gaping wound in his heart. The night was poisoned; neither the stars, nor the sea, nor the pearly necklace of streetlamps lighting the glittering curve of road could save him from the sharpness of this death. But this feeling only lasted for a moment—then the immanent reality of the revolution tore him out of his painful torpor. Morbid curiosity made him want to encounter this man whom Karim—full of hellish pride—placed higher than the oppressed people. If for only an instant he could confront him before Karim, he'd be able to destroy the idolatrous image set up in his comrade's mind. He'd expose the vanity, the nihilism, the false seductiveness of this perfidious soul, who wallowed in luxury while proclaiming subversion, like a magician at a fair. Maybe then Karim would understand that he was deluded, that all these stupid initiatives for overthrowing the government were destined to fail, and he'd return to the respectable precepts of real combat. The idea was wildly tempting. In fact, he had no choice: he needed Karim for a hazardous exploit—one the revolution demanded—things he hadn't dared to speak of yet. In his current state of mind Karim wouldn't even have stopped to listen. Taher summoned up all his powers of persuasion; he was going to employ a subtler tactic than those he used to inspire revolutionary faith in a roomful of the unemployed.

"I want you to do something for me," he said with surprising calm.

"What?"

"I'd like to meet this man you love so much. You and I go way back, and all I'm asking is for you to put me in touch with him—I want to speak with him."

Karim smiled slightly, and his face relaxed; the request visibly enchanted him.

"With pleasure," he said. "I'm sure that he'd like to meet you, too. You know, he's very open-minded. He's interested in every kind of human activity."

"I'm delighted to hear it," said Taher, surprised by how easy it had been (and smelling a trap). Can you take me to him tonight?

"If you like. You're in luck—I was planning to go see him. Taher, I hope that we can join forces again. I've never stopped thinking about you."


Just then the shadowy form of a patrolling policeman—he'd been slowly working his way along the length of the parapet—came to an abrupt halt in front of them. The two young men were startled. This representative of order looked like a hungry ogre in search of stray infants on the cliff road. They waited in silence for him to reveal the nature of their offense.

"Public assemblies are forbidden," he growled. "Go on, walk!"

"But there are only two of us," said Karim, delighted at this interruption.

"Two or a hundred, it's all the same, the policeman went on. Get going!"

He skulked away from them silently.

"Did you hear that son of a bitch!" Karim burst out.

"He's just a poor sucker following orders," said Taher. "It's not his fault that he doesn't know better. It's up to us to teach him."

"You really are crazy! Do you think I'm going to live a thousand years? I've only got one short life and you want me to spend it educating this gun-toting assassin?"

Taher shook his head sadly, like someone who no longer expects to be understood. He couldn't wait to see Heykal and tell him face-to-face just what he thought of him.

"Well, let's go," he said. "But first I have to take these shoes to the cobbler."

"At this time? Nothing's open."

"What do you think, that I'm going to leave my shoes with a capitalist cobbler! I have a friend who keeps his shop open all night—it's one of our meeting spots. It's not far from here; come with me."

Karim made a gesture of assent, then slipped his arm through Taher's and they set off. They crossed the road and made their way into the city's sordid depths, leaving behind the cliff and its enchanted scenery.

Once the introductions had been made, the three of them sat in Heykal's living room. They were silent, waiting for Siri, as slow and sleepy as ever, to serve them drinks. It took Siri a long, almost interminable time to acquit himself of his task, but nobody was paying any attention. They were too caught up with their extraordinary meeting to be distracted. Finally Siri set three glasses of rose water on the small low table, then left the room. But the silence refused to break.

Heykal observed Taher with the curiosity of an antiques dealer assessing a rare piece. He wasn't displeased by the visit; it was an opportunity to thoroughly examine this old friend of Karim's— one of the most dangerous revolutionaries in the city. He could tell Taher was ready to bite, but that he was still too polite to interrupt the silence with hostile words. He sat unhappily on the edge of his chair, as if ashamed to find himself in such contemptible company. There was no mistaking the glances he continued to shoot at Karim, as if holding him responsible for the whole painful situation. Heykal meant to wait patiently until Taher was thoroughly pre- pared to state his grievances. He was already fairly sure he knew what Taher had come all this way to find out, and he was curious to see him at work. What arguments would he bring to bear on Heykal's perfect serenity? In this confrontation of two concepts, different both in essence and application, Taher had already lost. He was out of his element. Heykal felt a twinge of pity; the fight was plainly unequal. What aberration had led this caveman, this violent fanatic, to think that he could come here and get away with provok- ing Heykal? What was the temptation? Heykal grew positively dizzy at the thought that this stubborn, spiteful revolutionary had been unable to resist the magnetism of his scorn. Conscious of his own influence, he felt a flash of tenderness for his visitor, as if Taher had come bringing love instead of hatred.

Taher's face bore an expression of manifest displeasure, even repul- sion; he was all shrunken up, like a man surrounded by rats. His comrade, the cobbler, had loaned him some sandals belonging to a client who had died, and his toes wiggled nervously under leather straps. He didn't know how to begin. He hadn't expected such a courteous reception, or the undeniable charm of his host, who, draped in his purple dressing gown, held court on the sofa across from him like a great lord receiving the respects of a humble visitor. Worst of all, Taher was conscious of his poverty, and for the first time in his life he felt the indignity of it. He was lost in this well- appointed bourgeois living room with its furniture gleaming with cleanliness, its gilded, red velvet–covered chairs in a hideous, out-dated style that were for him—having spent his whole life in slums and prisons—the height of affluence and leisure. What Taher objected to was this opulence, rather than the man who was hosting him in his house—for Heykal's ideas disconcerted him; he had to admit that he'd never encountered anyone like him. The man wasn't one of the executioners and he wasn't among the condemned. Somehow he fought power in his own way—a way that was an insult to those who paid for revolt with their blood. Taher couldn't imagine the possibility of a revolution that lacked a certain dose of hatred, and he was growing impatient, since Heykal appeared to be without a trace of the vengeful anger inherent in every oppressed being. He seemed to recognize the bloody-minded stupidity of the adversary and even to rejoice in it. Taher was exasperated by his host's calm simplicity; it offended his unflinching determination to fight or die. But maybe all this was only for show; maybe Heykal was just trying to seduce him, to lure him into his tenuous, fragile universe. Taher wasn't going to let that happen. The whole purpose of being there was to deflate the pretensions of this aristocrat with his insinuating charm. Karim was courting disaster, and he had to save him.

"Heykal effendi," he began. "I came here—"

"I know why you came," Heykal interrupted, speaking in a soft voice, raising his hand in a gesture of peace. "That can wait. First let me simply enjoy the pleasure of your company."

"What infinite generosity!" Taher resumed. "But that's enough for now, I'm sorry to say. What I want is an explanation. I've already told this turncoat"—he pointed at Karim—"just what I think of what you've done. It's a complete disaster. The police think we did it, and that's an insult to our honor as revolutionaries. What kind of game do you think you're playing?"

Heykal bore up under this brutal, but impulsively frank, attack with a smile of exquisite politeness. So Taher had come to defend his revolutionary honor! He didn't want the police to take him for a joker—that was all he cared about. And what ardor and enthusiasm his voice revealed when it came to the insult to his honor! He needed those criminals to respect him! How pathetic for a rebel! Even he couldn't break out of the vicious cycle of power. He played the game of honor and dishonor, just as he'd been taught to do. He'd never escape. He was more of a prisoner than a prisoner in a cell because he shared the same myths as his adversary; they grow and grow and surround everything like unbreakable walls. Heykal hoped that his gaze wasn't too visibly ironic; he didn't want to let his guest down.

"Games," he said, looking pensive. "You're right to talk about that. Because we're all playing a game, aren't we, Taher effendi? I profoundly regret that my game has given you offense and caused you trouble. But any man has the right to express his rebellion in his own way. Mine is what it is; at least it doesn't harm the innocent."

"How infantile!" Taher retorted disdainfully. "I don't doubt your intelligence, Heykal effendi, not in the least. But excuse me if I tell you that you're just having fun while the people are suffering from oppression. Fun is no way to fight. Violence must be met with violence. And forget about innocence!"

"Violence will never get to the bottom of this absurd world," Heykal responded. "That's just what these tyrants want: for you to take them seriously. To answer violence with violence shows that you take them seriously, that you believe in their justice and their authority, and it only builds them up. But I'm cutting them down."

"I don't see how! There is no historical basis to what you do—to your insipid farces!"

"How? It's easy. By letting the tyrants lead the way and being even stupider than they are. How far will they go? Well, I'll go farther. They'll have to prove themselves the greatest buffoons of all! And my pleasure will be that much greater."

"But the people!" cried Taher. "The poor people! You forget about them. They're not laughing!"

"Teach them to laugh," Taher effendi. "Now *that* is a noble cause."

"I don't know," said Taher in a strangled voice. "I've never learned to laugh. And I don't want to."

He said it regretfully, as if ending a painful and impossible love. Heykal felt his happiness melt away. It was true Taher didn't know how to laugh—one look at him and you could see it. In a state of constant tension about the battles to come, always plotting and scheming, worried out of his mind by the thought of the misery of the people—he was doomed to unhappiness. He was the perfect manager of the revolution. Nothing mattered apart from his job: that of a predestined savior, walled in by self-regard. Pure egotism! The worst kind of egotism, since by definition it depended on a multitude of other people—whole groups of people—in order to thrive and prosper!

"Well," Heykal said, "I'm afraid the tyrants will make a fool of you. One of you is going to be the butt of a joke."

"What nerve, Heykal effendi! Has it never occurred to you that we might actually defeat the tyrants?"

"I prefer a laughable tyrant to a dead one. The pleasure lasts longer."

Taher wrung his hands and squirmed in his chair, convulsed with shame. He was certain that Heykal's cynical paradox-mongering words were solely intended to humiliate him. Joy and pleasure—to dare to speak of such things to him, he who had known nothing but the exquisite pangs of hunger. Finally he was showing his true colors. Taher's shame turned into indignation at the intolerable thought that this man, disguised as an apostle of pacifism, had conquered Karim with his tricks. Karim had a generous heart; had he sunk to the point of becoming an impostor's accomplice? Taher glanced at his old comrade frantically, as if hoping for assistance in the name of some long-ago pact that no treachery could undo. But Karim appeared to take no note of his suffering. Almost gasping, a smile hovering on his lips, he had eyes only for Heykal, whose every word seemed to emerge from the mouth of an oracle. His subordination was complete. It made Taher sick.

"Don't you have anything to say, you traitor!"

Karim turned toward his comrade, cut to the quick, torn from the state of ecstasy into which Heykal's last reply had sent him.

"What am I supposed to say," he replied angrily. "I'm in complete agreement with Heykal. A child would understand what he just said. But you, you're deaf! You boast of your revolutionary honor like a pregnant woman displaying her belly! It's painful to watch."

"Look where your treachery has led you—you insult everybody you once held dear. You're worth less than a dog!"

"Taher effendi, do not condemn my friend Karim," interrupted Heykal. "Maybe he used to be different, but he has the right to change. Do you deny that thinking evolves?"

"But he doesn't think at all," exploded Taher. "He's a hypocrite; I understand that now. He pretended to love the people for the pleasure of making fun of them. He betrayed them and he betrayed me at the same time!"

"That's not fair," Heykal said. "Karim hasn't betrayed anyone. That would require a great deal of ambition—and Karim doesn't have any. He dreams of a life of love."

"So he says. But if I were you, I'd watch out. Did you know, Heykal effendi, that he told me he'd lay down his life for you if you asked him to? Crazy, no? And yet he was sincere. And he was sincere when he wanted to give his life to the revolution."

"It's not the same thing!" Karim yelled. "You're confusing everything, it's unbearable! My love for Heykal is free of politics. I don't love him to deliver him from oppression; he's already free. It has nothing to do with your kind of love—like an accountant distributing future happiness to the poor!"

Taher looked at Heykal with a mocking sneer.

"I'd like to know just what kind of man you are to inspire such passion in this cretin."

"A very simple man, Taher effendi. Only I never inflict my notion of honor and dignity on others. I look for other things from my fellow human beings. My friend Karim is free to change his way of thinking tomorrow. I wouldn't hold it against him, because no matter what he does, he'll never be a bore. Which is the important thing."

"So what do you think is important in a man?"

"That he gives me a sense of wonderful plenitude, even when caught up in life's trivialities. The breadth of joy he conveys. That's how you recognize the richness of a man's love."

The odious, detestable mania of the man! Talking about joy again! Did he really believe in it? Was that all there was for him on earth? On this ravaged earth, which men burn to ashes again and again— how could anyone find love and happiness here? You'd have to be a slob to settle for such inanities. Or a grinning idiot. But Heykal wasn't a slob or an idiot. He wanted to amuse people, to teach them how to laugh at the tyrants. Easy enough to say! But the people needed to learn other lessons. Taher thought about everything that remained to teach the people, and the immensity of the task made him sick with despair.

Heykal gave him a sympathetic glance, stirred to the depths to detect, in this model manager of the revolution, a budding awareness of the vanity of his struggle—barely budding, true, but appreciable all the same. The tight jacket, the stiff collar and threadbare tie were emblematic of his perfect domestication. The rags of a society that he wanted to fight against—he made it a point of pride to wear them. A revolutionary, but with dignity—dressed in the same uniform as the adversary and ready to take his place. What a magnificent specimen of the era! And ripe for reinvention still; Heykal would have liked to adopt him, to have him around all the time, the living image of irony. But it was a dream for a king—an object so precious was beyond his means.

The silence, and Heykal's affectionate gaze—as it seemed to Taher—made Taher get a grip on himself. He broke in:

"These virtues you speak of, Heykal effendi, could just as easily belong to a rat. Would you accept the breath of joy from a rat?"

"Rats kill any breath of joy," responded Heykal, "and whatever side they're on, I hate them. But that's not the kind of man you are, Taher effendi. I know how to recognize a man's true character, beneath the appearances. Why do you stubbornly put on a mask that makes you suffer? I'm sure you could learn to be happy and to embrace the frivolous and the vain. I'd like to see you when that happens."

Taher was growing confused, even as the full horror of the man's honeyed words dawned on him. That Heykal saw him as a frivolous man was the greatest conceivable insult to his fighter's pride. He averted his face as if to escape this badge of shame, and at last to understand how useless it was to argue with a shadow. He couldn't wait to get back to the world of iniquities that awaited him outside; there, at least, he might be defeated, but he was never unhappy.

Heykal lifted his glass of tepid rose water from the table and addressed his guest:

"To your health, Taher effendi!"

Taher appeared not to understand. Mechanically, he picked up his own glass, meaning to lift it to his lips, hesitated, then abruptly threw it on the floor. It smashed and he looked proud, almost arrogant—his dignity had been restored.

Karim was too stunned to react. He remained in his chair, waiting to see what Heykal would do. But Heykal was impassive, as if indifferent to his visitor's scandalous provocation. His face bore a look of indulgence. He even seemed to regard Taher with a certain respect.

Having heard the noise, Siri entered the room and, without a word, began to pick up the broken glass. Nobody spoke; they seemed to be waiting for Siri to finish cleaning up. When he finally left, Taher rose. For a moment he looked at Heykal. He gave a slight nod and slowly made his way to the door.

Heykal rose from the sofa and followed. For a few seconds, they hesitated at the door. Heykal said:

"The rose water was not poisoned, Taher effendi! It was offered in friendship."

Taher didn't respond. Suddenly Heykal grabbed him by the shoulders and pulled him close.

"Taher, my brother, you are brave, but you are lost. It's too bad!"

"Lost to whom?" asked Taher in a voice like a stifled cry.

"Lost to me, to me alone," said Heykal. "Now go. And may peace be with you."

Then he turned to Karim, who looked on, speechless.

THE LITTLE girl ate her ice cream while peering over it at Heykal; there was nothing coy about her look, which was somehow arch, timid, and discreet in a self-consciously feminine way. She sucked the spoon slowly—carefully attending to it with a kind of blissful gluttony. Heykal was pretending not to see; his love of seduction drove him to feign indifference even with a child. This one must be about eight years old; a big green ribbon was tied around the single braid that hung down her back. She was extremely beautiful, but not with the detestable beauty of the rich, well-fed children that Heykal loathed on first sight. Her features were refined and there was a profound sadness in her eyes; already the world had taken its toll. What had piqued Heykal's interest had been her childish melancholy, verging on despair. She was accompanied by her mother, a nagging battle-ax with foolishness written on her face, steeped in social status and exhibiting heavy gold bracelets on her arms. When she addressed her daughter, Heykal thought he saw the girl shrink up, as if ashamed to be associated with the ignoble creature seated across from her. Apparently the mother suspected her antagonism; her voice bore traces of that special hatred parents feel for rebellious children. Unconsciously she resented the girl for belonging to a different breed. This mother—Heykal would have liked to kill her, to see her disappear through a trapdoor. Horrible person! He suffered for this little girl and, given her complicitous look, he began to love her.

Customers were few in the luxurious tearoom, located in an elegant neighborhood, where Soad had asked to meet. There was the little girl and her mother, and apart from that just two other tables occupied by ladies gorging themselves on cake and blabbing quietly to each other. Heykal was nauseated by the women's voraciousness. He drank a mouthful of tea to keep from throwing up and resumed his silent dialogue with the young girl. He could tell that he intrigued her, that she felt a strange link uniting them. Inside he trembled to think that he had become the object of her childish imagination. What could she be thinking? Suddenly he'd had enough of feigned indifference; changing tactics, he stared straight at her. Quickly she lowered her eyes and a blush rose to her cheeks. Heykal relaxed. Then he had a crazy notion and felt a thrill of action: he'd take the girl by the hand and, right in front of her mother's horrified eyes, they'd walk out. He was sure that she would do it.

The girl's eyes grew even sadder; they looked misty with tears. Did she suspect that he wanted to save her, to tear her away from her monstrous mother? She seemed to be waiting for a sign from Heykal to get up and follow him. But he knew it was all a fantasy. He'd never give in to the wild desire that took hold of him whenever he saw a child of his own kind in the company of unworthy parents. He smiled regretfully at the little girl. And—extraordinary thing— she seemed to understand, for she bowed her head slightly, looking sweeter yet. Heykal's heart fluttered, and he closed his eyes to savor her innocence and her divine understanding.

Suddenly Soad was standing in front of him. Heykal didn't recognize her right away; she'd changed. She was wearing her hair in a high bun; her eyes were blackened with kohl and she'd put on lipstick. She carried herself like a lady, and there was an unexpected hardness about her features—quite a disguise. Heykal noticed something even more surprising: the girl was wearing expensive earrings with large precious stones. He didn't comment, as she clearly expected him to do.

She sat across from him and, for a moment, she staged a grotesque scene, like someone in a silly mask making wild faces in order to be recognized. But Heykal maintained a detached, almost cold attitude; he seemed altogether unaware of her transformation. Vexed by this lack of curiosity, she glanced around in the hopes of exciting some public admiration, only to be disappointed by the lack of customers; she turned back to the young man. She could no longer resist asking:

"How do I look?"

"Superb!" Heykal responded. "You remind me of my grandmother!"

She pouted like a sulky little girl, a look that didn't suit her new brand of beauty at all—she could tell right away from Heykal's icy glance. She had just voluntarily crossed the border that separated her from childhood; from now on, she would no longer be able to move him. She was a woman now, and she knew how well he was defended against the ploys and the duplicity of her sex.

She stopped pouting and said in the tone of a poised and very confident young woman:

"Be nice to me. I have some fantastic news for you."

"Tell me. I'm listening."

"It happened today. The governor came to see my father, and they had a terrible fight. I heard everything. The governor still can't believe that my father has nothing to do with that business about the statue; he blames him for the situation."

"He has good reason to be furious," said Heykal. "You can't hold that against him."

"He has an even better reason to be furious—though you don't know it: the governor has at most a week left. The prime minister summoned him and demanded his resignation. Happy?"

Heykal pondered the news. He was surprised that he didn't really feel any joy. It was more like a sense of emptiness now that the governor was gone—as if someone had taken away his toy, a special toy that only he knew how to play with and only he could really enjoy. For a while the governor had been the bottomless source of his every earthly delight. His salvation! He was the sap that made Heykal's critical spirit grow and thrive. Heykal dreaded that he would be replaced by some mid-level bureaucrat, a petty tyrant without any aspirations, lacking even the absurd fantasies of his predecessor; the banality of tyrants was even more disheartening than their crimes. A period of mediocrity and boredom—that's where things were headed—one lousy choice among the various candidates for governor and it would all be over. Heykal groaned inwardly to think that his future pastimes hung by a thread of chance. But there it was.

Soad looked at him with enormous eyes; she was expecting a triumphant outburst. She couldn't understand his silence.

"Why don't you say something?"

"Well, that's an exceptional piece of news. I'm sorry. You deserve a reward."

He reached across the table, took her hand, and gave it a polite kiss. That was when he saw the giant topaz ring on her finger—an extraordinary jewel that leaped out at him like a flash of light in darkness. But he betrayed no surprise as he set the young woman's hand down on the table. The ring was like a living thing, and Soad gazed at it with hideous delight. Without turning her head from the brilliant stone she murmured:

"Aren't you surprised to see me with this ring?"

"Why surprised?"

"Oh, I know! Nothing surprises you! You don't care about me. But I'm so unhappy!"

"Unhappy? With all that jewelry?"

"I haven't told you everything. In this thing with the governor—I'm the real victim."

"What do you mean?"

"Well, my father acted suspicious about that check. He must have inquired about it at the newspaper you sent it to. He didn't say anything to me about it, not explicitly at least, but he keeps going on about how badly I've treated him."

"And that's why you're unhappy?"

"No, but now he wants to get rid of me. He demands that I get married. Now that's a terrible punishment, you have to agree."

"But what does the jewelry have to do with it?"

"Well, I didn't compromise. I told him I didn't want to get married. He started off by threatening terrible things, and then to bring me around, he gave me all the jewelry that after my mother died had been locked away to give to me when I was older. But it was time, he'd decided, for me to look like a marriageable woman; he wants his future son-in-law to appreciate the fortune that I'll bring."

"He's quite right. He understands the kind of man he's dealing with. You should rest easy: you'll find a husband before you know it."

"So you aren't sorry for me?"

"Don't play the victim. You're perfectly happy to get married."

"What choice do I have, since *you* don't want me?"

"I don't like jewelry," said Heykal, in a cutting voice.


And so the idyll had reached its end—the most ridiculous end imaginable. Heykal hadn't had any expectations, and he felt no disappointment. Everything was falling into place. A few jewels, and the love-struck little girl was gone, leaving nothing but a woman with an attachment to comfort and money, to the security that comes from material possessions. All of a sudden she'd given up doing things for fun and had gone back to her rotten world. The truth was, her only way forward was through trickery. Trickery was her element; she'd been born to it. And that was how she would succeed in employing her talents, assuaging her thirst for possessions, and triumphing again and again over men.

Heykal would have liked to shed a few tears for this girl whom he'd been so close to and who was now about to disappear from his life, but his eyes remained dry. The pain was good, almost like joy. He felt that he'd been reborn, free and clear, with all his restored richness intact. He looked over at the other little girl—the one who still hated her mother—searching her face for a trace of that innocent spontaneity that had been taken from him. She'd finished her ice cream and was sitting with her elbows on the table, one hand under her cheek, a brooding expression on her face. Heykal thought she was sulking, and he smiled at the thought that already she was jealous.

"But how can I?" whimpered Soad. "How can I even talk to another man, now that I've known you! I mean, not only because I love you but because I'll be bored to death. You're the only man who doesn't disgust me!"

He knew that it wasn't true, that she'd adapt easily to the ugly world she was returning to. The ugliness wouldn't even offend her as it would be hidden under brilliant costumes and masks. Soon all of the people trailing along behind her would seem charming to her; she'd never see the horror behind the smiling faces that her beauty had conquered. Heykal knew all about the puerile vanity of women who're only bored when the adoration stops. Soad was too beautiful to ever be bored.

What was the point of disabusing her? She'd played her part willingly and well. And the passion with which she had offered up to him the treasures of her young body was also worthy of esteem. He should be indulgent of her incoherence and her fears; he wasn't an ingrate. She still deserved a touch of tenderness.

"I taught you how to find joy everywhere," he said. "So don't worry; you won't be bored."

"Will you think of me?" she asked. Then, worried: "But not in your mocking way! I know you!"

"I will think of you entirely seriously. I promise."

They were silent for a moment, then Soad opened her bag and began to reapply her lipstick. Heykal was struck by the look of contentment with which she completed the task. He'd never seen her do it before, making that thoroughly obscene gesture of stroking a red wand over her parted lips. She seemed proud of the act, as if it made her a woman. Disgust and a hint of bitterness seized him at the sight of this sacrilegious daubing: it disfigured the image he wished to preserve of the girl. He turned away, waiting for the barbaric work to be done.

When she was finally ready, he stood. They left the tearoom and said their goodbyes in the street.

As for Heykal, he trembled with his new freedom, already alert to the promises that lay strewn in his path. Other faces, other passions awaited, and he contemplated the end of his love with a voluptuous serenity. It was always like this. He would feel a strange happiness, as if the woman he'd abandoned had left with a portion of his love, so that a part of him would always be out there roaming the vast universe.

The busy, crowded street reminded him that as yet nobody knew about the important event—the governor's resignation—that would soon take place. Heykal suddenly was filled with delight: he had to tell his friends right away. He picked up his pace, looking to see if he could find the jasmine seller who was usually somewhere around here. At last he saw him, standing by a door, unshaven, a sinister figure in spite of the red flower tucked behind his ear to signal his profession. Heykal bought a slender bouquet of jasmine, slipping it delicately into the inside pocket of his jacket. Then he hailed a horse-drawn coach and yelled Urfy's address to the driver.

Seated at his desk in the empty classroom, Urfy was concentrating with difficulty on the book he was reading. The late-afternoon light still penetrated the basement windows, but it was the stingy, dirty light of a dungeon. Urfy abandoned his reading, removed his glasses, and rubbed his eyes irritably. The thoughts rattling around in his head filled him with bitterness. It was his mother, as always, who was worrying him; he dreaded the decision he had to make. One of his friends, a doctor, had strongly advised him to put the old woman in a clinic where she would receive state-of-the-art care. There was a slim chance that her condition might improve—but was a slim chance worth the anguish of separation? The clinic was fairly distant from the city, and he would be able to visit her only rarely. It was a proposal that Urfy stubbornly rejected. Transferring his mother into the care of strangers would feel like abandonment. Little by little, she'd start to forget him: his image would vanish into the folds of her wavering memory and in the end he would be extinct in her heart. And this flame that still burned in his mother's spirit, the last trace of the happiness of his childhood, was his only safeguard against an atrocious world. He suppressed the tears that were rising to his eyes and put his glasses back on. When he was ready to start reading again, he realized that the light had disappeared and he could no longer see a thing.

Heykal's arrival in the classroom startled him—as if he were an enemy who had sprung out of the darkness to attack. Heykal was the last person he wanted to see, since he more than anyone couldn't have cared less about the situation. Heykal's humor and irony would force Urfy to behave in a way that was incompatible with the torture he was undergoing. He needed calm and solitude. But he overcame his feelings of revulsion at the intrusion, and descended from the podium to greet his guest.

"Welcome," he said.

"Hello," Heykal responded. "I'm sorry to disturb you, but I had to see you."

"You're not disturbing me at all," Urfy said quickly. "I was just reading, but I noticed it was getting too dark. Wait here, and I'll go get a light."

"Oh, no!" protested Heykal. "It's fine like this. We don't need a light."

Urfy didn't insist. His visitor's desire corresponded exactly to his own wish to remain in the dark. What he was most afraid of was that Heykal, with his sharp eye, would discern his distress. He didn't want to talk about his mother, not at any price, and he didn't want to discuss the horrible dilemma he faced. This was his own private ordeal, a sacred destiny, and he would hate to see his pain picked over by impious hands. But as soon as he smelled the odor of jasmine emanating from the young man he knew that he wouldn't escape the thing he feared most. He knew Heykal's crazy ways. The bouquet was in the inside pocket of his jacket; he was sure to take it out at some point to offer it to the old madwoman. He must be intending to visit her in her room. These meetings between Heykal and his mother terrified Urfy. There was something bizarre, almost insane, about them. It strained his nerves terribly—already he trembled at the prospect.

"Sit down," he said, indicating one of the benches and taking a seat across the aisle. "I hope it isn't bad news that brings you."

"On the contrary. Urfy, my brother, it's a time to rejoice! The governor is ruined."

"It's in the papers?"

"Not yet. But the news came from a reliable source. You can believe me."

"What happened?"

"It's very simple. As I predicted, the prime minister demanded his resignation. In a week, we'll be rid of him."

Urfy didn't feel like rejoicing. What did the governor's ruin matter to him; it couldn't make up for his own ruin. He could find nothing to say that suggested happiness, or even satisfaction. Everything in him was inert; everything boiled down to suffering. But he mustn't disappoint Heykal by keeping silent. And yet in spite of his efforts his voice was bitter when he spoke:

"It's everything you hoped for, isn't it?"

Heykal seemed not to have heard; his face remained immobile as it slowly disappeared into darkness. By now Urfy could barely make out his features, and he was growing ever more uncomfortable. What if he burst into laughter? He shuddered at the thought. Instantly he knew that Heykal was in an unusual state of mind; something indefinable and vaguely worrisome was going on within him. Urfy leaned across the aisle, reducing the distance that separated him from his friend, presenting his ear, as if in expectation of a whispered message.

"In a sense, yes," Heykal finally replied.

"What do you mean?"

"I mean, my dear Urfy, that the future may hold some surprises for us. We can't forget that there are mediocre governors, whose tasteless tyranny wouldn't give us anything to work with."

"No doubt," Urfy said, a bit disconcerted by Heykal's odd way of thinking. "Leave it to chance then—I suppose it's served us well so far. We've had a lucky streak. We've got nothing to complain about."

"I'm not complaining. But I have a feeling the next governor will bore us to death. He might even try to act sensible—to make people forget the foolishness of his predecessor. He'll be out to prove himself, that we can be sure of. Perhaps we'll have to go into exile."

Urfy had made a superhuman effort to appear interested in Heykal's premature anxiety about the next governor, and now he began to wonder if Heykal hadn't perhaps sensed some of his inner turmoil. Why, in any case, was he going on about wanting to leave for other, even more respectable places? Urfy didn't need to go abroad to find madness and misery. They were flourishing right here in the basement, a daily challenge to his reason. There was plenty for him to get excited about at home, and maybe Heykal envied him for that. He feared the face of his friend, eager to discover the symptoms of this strangely perverse jealousy. But Heykal's mocking smile, floating in semidarkness, grew suddenly clearer, and Urfy realized that this man, who was incapable of feeling pity, was making fun of him.

The smile disappeared. Heykal asked him:

"How's your mother? It's been a long time since I've seen her."

"Still the same."

"There's no hope of a turn for the better?"

This was pure nastiness, and Urfy regained his presence of mind. Heykal could only be inquiring for his own benefit. No doubt he dreaded any alteration in the old lady's condition; he wanted her just as she was, crushed by illness and all for his own pleasure.

Urfy was overcome with a desire to set a trap for Heykal. Maybe at last he'd unmask this solicitude that was more torturous than the vilest indifference.

"I've been advised to send her to a clinic," he said. "But I'm reluctant to do it."

"Of course."

"But in the end I'll probably agree."

"Don't!" Heykal cried. Urfy had never seen him so passionate.

"Don't ever leave her, brother! What can you expect from those people? It's like a death sentence!"

"She needs care that I can't give her. They use new methods in this clinic. They told me that she might get better."

"You're like a child! If they knew how to restore her sanity why wouldn't they apply their methods to all of humanity! No. Nothing can cure her. They'll treat her disgustingly—and just for their filthy experiments. She'll suffer."

"You don't think she suffers now?"

"If you really want to know, no—she has no notion of suffering. We're the ones who see what she is going through; we're the ones who suffer."

"What! Heykal, you suffer?"

Heykal reached out to touch the schoolmaster's arm in a gesture of supplication.

"Don't abandon her to those brutes! It would be monstrous!"


Heykal fell quiet and turned away. How could he have succumbed to such weakness? Now that the panic passed, now that he was relieved of his fear of never seeing the old madwoman again, of losing her forever, he regretted his words and the passion with which he'd pronounced them. What would Urfy think? He could almost sense the schoolmaster's stupefied, watchful gaze, while his own face was lost in the heavy darkness of the classroom. All he could see were the letters of the alphabet inscribed on the blackboard, like luminous hieroglyphs. Then, slowly, as if magically commanded by them, he got up, walked down the aisle, and climbed onto the podium, to sit at the schoolmaster's desk. Far away, below him, he could make out Urfy, a vague mass bent over and caught in the darkness. It seemed as if thousands of years had passed since he'd revealed his secret, and he could look him in the face now, certain of being understood.

The stupor that had overcome Urfy gradually turned into joy. He regained all his confidence, and he wanted to proclaim his delight at the discovery that Heykal was so close to him in his suffering. The ignominious pain was gone now that he knew Heykal, too, was touched by the wound that tore at his soul. And yet as always the other man kept his distance, still imprisoned in his pride. What was he doing up there on the podium, like some forlorn creature stranded on a rock? Why didn't he come close and take his hand in brotherhood? Urfy attempted to speak but the words stuck in his throat, and it was Heykal's voice that rang out in the silence.

"May I see her?"

"She would be enchanted," Urfy said. Come on.

He waited for Heykal to join him, then left the classroom with him and walked down the corridor that led to the madwoman's room.

The door was open and a faint light shone within. Urfy paused on the threshold, worried. He didn't see his mother anywhere in the room. It was a sort of cell, with a high window that was boarded up tight—to prevent the crazy old woman from attracting the attention of snooping neighbors. It contained a little iron bed, a chest of drawers, and a small sofa covered in jute; on the floor was a straw mat. An oil lamp, set on the chest of drawers, was the source of the meager light.

"Mother!" Urfy called.

There was no response, but Urfy sensed movement in the corner between the bed and the wall. He drew near, followed by Heykal. The old lady was crouched on the ground, seemingly busy patching some rags that were spread over her knees. She showed no surprise at their arrival; it was as if they'd always been there. But her dim eyes brightened at the sight of Heykal, animating her wasted face.

"I waited for you, my prince!" she said. "I dreamed of you all last night. You were on a white horse and you were slaying a dreadful dragon. But after each of your blows the dragon was reborn: it wouldn't die. And you, prince, you laughed and laughed ... And I knew why you laughed. Deep down, you didn't want to kill the dragon; the dragon entertained you too much for you to want it dead."

"Mother," said Urfy. "Get up, and go lie down on your bed."

But not until Heykal leaned over and held out his hand to help her would she move. She gripped his hand and rose to her feet as nimbly as a young girl, agile and full of grace. Her cotton dress revealed how skinny she was, and she was as light as a feather. She reached up to arrange the thin white threads of her hair, and, grown strangely coquettish all of a sudden, stretched out languorously on the bed—a pose that was both naive and shockingly shameless— like a courtesan awaiting the tributes of her admirers.

Now Heykal pulled the bouquet of jasmine from the inside pocket of his jacket and offered it to her. She took it and lifted it to her nostrils, breathing the perfume of the flowers with the elegance of a woman in the habit of receiving such attentions.

"Prince, you spoil me!" she simpered. "You'll ruin yourself, for an old woman like me!"

"It's nothing, a trifle compared to the happiness you give me," responded Heykal.

"Happiness—me?! Prince, you're mocking my old age!"

"You know that I would never dare to do that."

"But I can tell that you're a man with a taste for mockery."

"Under far different circumstances, perhaps. Here, my heart overflows with gratitude."

"Your heart is big, prince. It requires vast spaces. What do you see in this miserable hole! There are marvels outside. Why do you come to waste your time here?"

She waved the jasmine in the air like a fan, and the rank room began to smell sweet. Heykal sat at her feet, at the end of the bed. He seemed to be unaware of Urfy's presence and was watching the old woman with peaceful joy.

"There's nothing out there that you could possibly be missing," he said. "You must believe me."

Suddenly she shut her eyes—she seemed to have fallen into a state of intense meditation. With her head thrown back on the pillow, she pressed the bouquet of jasmine hard against her nostrils as if she was breathing in the scent of the world outside, the world of the living, and trying to remember it.

Urfy struggled against a feeling of unreality. He was standing be-hind Heykal, and over his shoulder he could see his mother stretched out on her bed like a corpse. He didn't dare intervene in what seemed to him to be a gift from heaven. By what miracle was Heykal able to carry on such a conversation with his mother? He spoke to her naturally, as if she was sane, and the old lady responded in the same way, as if the sheer magic of his presence had made her disordered mind begin to function. Right then Urfy began to won-der if his mother was really crazy or if she had been playing a part. But he banished the question from his mind; what was most impor-tant for now was to see her emerging from the darkness to regain her dignity and good humor.

The old lady opened her eyes, lowered the bouquet, and asked, a little anxiously:

"How is humanity these days, prince? I remember it as being nasty."

She seemed to be asking about a foreign country she had once visited in her youth but to which she'd never returned.

"It still is," responded Heykal. "But human foolishness remains entertaining enough."

"There's no hatred in you. I could tell in my dream the other night. I didn't see a single spark of meanness in your eyes when you were fighting the dragon. And yet he wanted to devour you, prince. I would never have gotten over it. Be careful."

"I won't let myself be eaten up. I'm not the type. I know how to defend myself, even without hatred. Don't worry about me."

She gripped his hand and brought it to her lips, like a woman crushed by her lover's departure for a pointless war.

"Yes, defend yourself. And come back victorious!"

Heykal contemplated her, touched to previously unsuspected depths of his being by this emaciated but smooth face, unwrinkled even by age. He knew no face so transparent, so utterly without blemish. Even the face of the little girl in the tearoom now seemed to bear a stigma of impurity. Her animation had been founded on guile and will, born of unflinching determination to seduce a cunning adversary—already she displayed the tools of her femininity. But the peace of this moment was something else entirely. Saved! Yes, he was saved from the oppressive hypocrisy of men. Only opposite this madwoman, who had forgotten the torments of vanity and lucre, could he feel at peace with the world. For him she had become the incarnation of a human being free of rancor or ambition.

He could see that the old woman was also observing him with an expression of happiness, as if she couldn't believe the marvelous peace she was feeling.

"We understand each other, don't we, prince?"

"Yes," said Heykal. "But it's our secret and we mustn't tell anyone."

Then she leaped from the bed and began to skip and spin around in the narrow space between the bed and the dresser. Her dress flared away from her feeble body, revealing her skinny brown-spotted legs, as she began a melancholy chant that was nonetheless full of spirit and youth, and her voice was that of a young girl happily playing in the garden of her childhood.

Heykal didn't make a move to stop this spontaneous outbreak of dancing. He was happy watching her, delighted; the scene seemed as beautiful to him as a supernatural vision.

Urfy blanched; for a moment, he'd wanted to intervene, to interrupt the charm of this wild dance that was leading his mother back into madness. But as he observed Heykal, something shifted. He understood that madness and its ways held nothing terrifying. He could live as easily with his mother as with any human being. Madness makes no difference. He seized onto this as if it were his salvation, and, looking at his mother, he began to smile.

The old lady abruptly stopped spinning. Gasping, she curled up on her bed, her features ecstatic.

"Little one," she said, addressing her son. "Buy me a new dress. A dress with sequins. I want to look good the next time the prince comes to visit. He gives me flowers, and I receive them like a beggar. I must be beautiful."

She reached out and grasped the bouquet of jasmine. Her head fell back on the pillow and she slept deeply.

The two men watched for a moment, then left the room in silence.

Urfy was afraid to speak; never in his life had he been so happy. An enormous burden seemed to slide off his shoulders, leaving him free and invulnerable. He no longer stooped but held his head high as he followed Heykal to the front door.

Before parting they shook hands. They stood in the deserted, badly lit street in front of the basement door.

"You have a precious gift," said Heykal. "Don't ever give her up to those criminals!"

"Don't worry," responded Urfy. "I understand now. And forgive me, Heykal, my brother, that it took so long."

Heykal walked off, then turned back to see Urfy still standing in front of the basement entrance. Once again he waved, with all the pomp and circumstance of a king departing for exile, leaving all that is most precious to him far behind.

# 12

IT WAS only a big cloud passing over the city, but it blotted out the sun so completely you would have thought a storm was brewing. The kite was a yellow streak against the dark background of sky, and it pitched back and forth, tossed by a gusty sea breeze. The long fringed tail wriggled and writhed like a snake sprung from the belly of the cloud into a maddening void. Karim grasped the string firmly, racing around the terrace, back and forth, maneuvering the kite to ever greater heights. It was a new kite, with an enormous tail, and he was testing it with fierce pleasure—he'd made it for Amar, the little prostitute who'd shown up again the night before. When he came home, he'd found her sitting on the steps of his building. She'd apologized for disturbing him, but Karim had lifted her in his arms and carried her to the bedroom. He made love to her all night, and in the morning he wanted to give her something. But what? He had no money, nothing of any value to express his gratitude. Then he thought he'd make a kite—not for financial consideration but as a pure disinterested work of art. He leaped out of bed and got started, choosing his materials with care, as if getting ready to build a palace for the woman of his dreams.

Now he was waiting for the kite to scale the heights, to anchor itself firmly in the sky, before calling the girl to come see. He was proud of himself; it was a triumph of kite-making and she was sure to admire his skill. Wasn't it a marvelous gift—so pretty, this kite sailing through the stormy immensity of the sky like a shimmering sign of love? He smiled at his silly romanticism, carefully steering the heavy kite through the unpredictable dangers of the atmosphere.

He was worried, fearing an accident; a moment's distraction and his beautiful gift might split to pieces. For a moment he panicked, then sighed with relief; his task was done. High in the sky the kite hung still, solitary and regal; Karim could feel it vibrating at the end of its string. He stopped, out of breath, his bare chest glistening with sweat, and leaned on the parapet. For a long moment, he stood admiring his creation with childlike pride.

"Dear God! I can see you're having fun!"

Karim gave a start, and the kite pitched lightly in the distance; he tugged on the string to steady it. He knew that voice, and without taking his eyes from the kite, he yelled out:

"Hello, Taher! Believe me, I'm not having fun, I'm hard at work!"

Taher strode onto the terrace. He wore his signature tight suit, starched collar, and tie. But this time he wasn't barefoot; his shoes had new soles, very thick, made to last a long time. They made an imposing sound on the terrace. The sound seemed to give Taher pleasure; with each step his self-confidence grew. He approached Karim and put his hand on the young man's shoulder.

"Delighted to see you at work," he said. "Your terrace is splendid, I have to admit. Listen, I have to apologize for the other night. Your friend Heykal knew what I meant, but you I need to talk to."

"No need to talk," said Karim.

He didn't look at Taher, keeping his eyes on the kite. The fat cloud had drifted off and now the sun reappeared, blurry, as if enfeebled by a long absence. Its rays glanced off the yellow framework of the kite, which sparkled in the sky like a trail of gold. Karim was ecstatic to be holding all this gold at the end of a string, but his ecstasy was tempered by more realistic concerns. Taher's presence on the terrace was not particularly to his liking; on the contrary, it was seriously worrying for him. Taher was putting him in a difficult, perhaps even a dangerous situation. The presence of a patented revolutionary in his home could cause no end of trouble, for no doubt the police were following his old friend's every movement. If by a stroke of bad luck they found out about this visit, they'd cause problems for him, the cruelest of which would be to make him move out. They would drive him out; no question of it. But what to do? He couldn't forbid Taher to enter his home; that would be improper and completely incompatible with his character. He had a highly developed sense of hospitality, and whatever might happen, he knew he could never bring himself to show his old friend the door.

Taher seemed annoyed by the offhandedness of his reception; he supposed Karim had no time for anything except his kite.

"Forget the kite and look at me," he said.

"It took me an hour to get it so high," said Karim, with eyes still lifted up. "Don't you think it's beautiful?"

"I'm in no mood to marvel at a kite. Who do you think I am? Come on, stop fooling around, I have serious things to discuss."

"God, what have I done!" lamented Karim. "There are a million men in this city, and you have to come to *me* with serious things to discuss! Can't you just enjoy yourself? Look at this kite, what a marvel!"

"The only reason I came to you is because this is your terrace," Taher remarked enigmatically.

"My terrace! You want to buy it?"

"Don't be ridiculous. I just want to make use of it this evening between nine and ten o'clock. That's all I ask."

"To do what? To sleep with a woman? If that's what you want, I'm happy to let you use my bedroom."

Without responding, Taher lifted his head to look at the kite, which remained perfectly still in the sky. He'd almost exhausted his patience for capturing Karim's attention; to make him understand his plan would be even more complicated. This fool thinks he's an engineer because he can fly a kite! Such degeneracy was beyond remedy, and Taher realized he was up against what he hated most: a joker and his wiles. How was he going to reach him? How could he penetrate his conscience when he was so proud to reject both dignity and honor, those treasures of the soul that even the most miserable beggar held fast beneath his rags? There Karim stood like a dim-witted child, mesmerized by his kite, while the people were suffering and the city stank with the sickness of their pain. Taher wanted to cry, to scream, to lash out, but he contained his rage: he was the people's proxy, the military wing of their revenge. Duty commanded that he forget his bitterness for now. He must focus on the reason he was here.

"Did you know that there's a big gala going on tonight at the casino?" he said in a soft, almost friendly tone, as if he hoped Karim would accompany him to the party.

"I didn't, in fact. I'm not as social as you think."

"It's not about being social. I abhor social events, as you well know. But the governor is going; he's the host of the party."

"So?" Karim asked, suddenly worried at this mention of the governor.

"He'll pass by in his car, with his motorcycle escorts—right down there on the cliff road. It's the only possible route. I've studied it."

"Where are you going with this? I'm not following."

Taher took his time before responding. He looked at Karim's tense features, his hand gripping the kite string. And then he said, quickly:

"It's very simple. I'll be here with a bomb and I'll throw it at his car. There's no better location."

"So we're back to that!" cried Karim, turning to Taher with horror in his eyes. "I was sure there would be a bomb somewhere in this!"

The neglected kite lurched violently and plunged several meters, like a crashing plane. Karim sprinted across the terrace, forgetting Taher, forgetting the insane plan he'd just been told, thinking of nothing but saving his kite from catastrophe. He gestured wildly, waving his arms in one direction and then another; then, with one quick, precise motion he set the kite back on course. He stood in the middle of the terrace, proud of this demonstration of his skills in aerial navigation.

"Bravo!" Taher called out. "I can't believe your incredible escape! It was amazing, I swear!"

Taher's flattery was so blatantly charged with ulterior motives that Karim felt disgusted. Without turning around he responded:

"My dear Taher, you know I'll never participate in such a violent act. My terrace is not a slaughterhouse."

"You can't refuse me," Taher said, and he came closer. "Plus, it's not just me you'd be refusing but all of our old friends. You know I speak for them, too."

Karim smiled to himself. With his tight suit, starched collar, and tie, Taher claimed to be a humble agent; he wanted Karim to know that an entire organization—the whole people, even—stood behind him, speaking through his very mouth. He wanted to impress him with the vast extent of his decision. Did he take him for a fool? Karim pitied his naiveté; he was certain that Taher had spoken to nobody about his plan. He knew him all too well: his taste for mystery and the insufferable obsession that led him to think of himself as entirely alone in the fight against injustice and oppression. Not ambition but something worse drove him, a sense that the sufferings of humanity were all his own. He planned to commit an act of unprecedented violence that would send him straight to the gallows, and he was marching toward it like a blind man toward an abyss—as if he'd been marked from birth for this and had no choice but to see it through. Of course he had no idea that the governor had already been defeated, that he was about to kill a man who was, for all intents and purposes, dead.

"Listen closely," said Karim. "The governor is out. He'll be gone in a matter of hours; the prime minister has demanded his resignation. Soon he'll be nothing but a memory. I have this from a reliable source."

"Don't give me your stories," Taher retorted suspiciously. "Your sources are a joke. You want me to believe that your posters brought him down?"

"Yes, our posters. I know it's hard for you to accept. But I'm begging you, give up your plan."

"Never. The decision is made: we will strike hard. The tyrant will die, mark my words. And you're going to help us."

He didn't say it, but he'd thought up the whole scene solely in order to wash off the filth that Heykal, with his quirks and jokes, had covered him with. Heykal, that impudent destroyer of revolutions. That the police suspected *him*, Taher, of being the author of such a travesty gnawed at him like a poison. How was he to continue his work as a militant? The false imputation paralyzed his every thought. He had to prove to the authorities that he hadn't renounced his methods, that he was still a force to be reckoned with; above all he couldn't allow them to sleep peacefully in the blissful confidence that they were up against a bunch of juvenile delinquents. He wanted to shake them up with an act of brutality that would make them understand that the posters, and that whole business about the governor's statue, had nothing to do with *his* ideas about overthrowing power. After this attack, they'd be forced to admit their mistake. How else was he to save the honor of his party in the eyes of the police—for Taher, in his own bloodthirsty way, was vain.

"You'd better not count on me," Karim said, beginning to reel in the kite by tugging on the string and winding it around his wrist. "I'll never agree to your scheme."

"It is not my scheme!" Taher cried out, furiously. "We're talking about the people! Don't you love the people anymore?"

"I don't love my own mother," replied Karim, annoyed. "Why do I have to love the people?"

"You're acting like an idiot. Admit that you're afraid."

"Of course I'm afraid. What do you think? I *like* my life!"

"This is what you call a life?" said Taher, pointing to the kite.

"It might seem strange to you," said Karim, smiling. "But for me, flying a kite is enough to make me happy. The governor does not interest me, apart from the fact that his foolishness makes me laugh. Why would I want him dead? I hate funerals."

He continued to wind the string around his wrist, slowly bringing the kite down. Taher watched with fierce, cold hatred. This insolence of Karim's was suffocating him; to conquer his indignation, he remained focused on his terrible mission. His one reason for living and for dying was now the attack on the governor. There was no humiliation and no indignity that he would not undergo to attain his glorious goal. To insist and to persuade—that was his role as a militant; and he was prepared to throw himself at Karim's feet and beg for his assistance, turncoat and traitor though he was. Karim no longer meant anything to him, he'd torn him out of his heart for good; he was just a tool that Taher had to make use of in order to settle his score with the governor.

The kite was descending upon them, like an enormous wounded bird, resplendent in the sun. Karim brought it down skillfully, then ran over to pick it up and stash it in the corner of the terrace.

Just then, Taher caught glimpse of something: what was this, a mirage? some sort of vision perfectly designed to seduce him and squash all his vengeful zeal? He stood there, shocked and furious, staring at the girl who was in the doorway of Karim's bedroom. It was Amar, the little prostitute, who'd come out in search of her lover but, seeing a stranger on the terrace, had then retreated. She was as shocked as he was. She'd taken a bath and appeared cool and elegant, and her young body, glimpsed through the thin fabric of her dress, made her uncannily desirable. Taher averted his eyes with disgust, as if from the very image of debauchery and corruption.

"You live with a woman now!" he thundered at his friend.

"She's my mistress," said Karim. "Come on, let me introduce you."

"I don't want to. She must have heard our conversation!"

"Don't worry about that. She won't denounce you. She's one of the governor's victims. His ordinances prevent her from soliciting."

"This kind of victim means nothing to me! She means nothing—she's just the trash of our oppressive social system!"

"What!" roared Karim. "You think she's trash! But she has the most beautiful breasts in the world! I'd be perfectly happy with trash like this."

Only a second earlier, Taher had still held out a faint hope of convincing Karim, but after seeing this girl with all her vestal allure he knew it was hopeless—the man was a slave to lust. The girl controlled him with sex. He was a wreck drifting in the cesspool of the regime. Not even as a doormat could he serve the revolution.

"I'm going," he said. "Not that I've wasted my time. You've shown me just how low a man can sink."

"Wait!" called Karim. "I'm about to make some coffee. Won't you have a cup?"

He'd just realized that he'd broken all the rules of hospitality by offering nothing to Taher; he was sincerely ashamed.

But Taher didn't turn around to accept or refuse his invitation; the sound of his thick soles rang down the stairway, vanishing forever.

Amar walked across the terrace to her lover.

"Who was that guy? He was scary."

"He makes bombs," Karim replied.

"Bombs!" The girl was stunned. "What an awful day!"

"On the contrary, it's a marvelous day!"

He put his arm around her shoulder and returned to the bedroom, holding her tight. After all that fuss about bombs, he wanted to make love.

———

The next day around noon Heykal opened the paper that his servant had brought him and learned about the governor's assassination.

The picture on the front page showed the governor's car ripped apart by the explosion; there was also a photo of Taher, his face swollen and bloody, his handcuffed fists held out in front of him in a gesture of supreme dignity. The details of the attack filled several pages, but Heykal read no farther. He crumpled the paper and threw it on the floor. He was appalled by the gratuitous violence. The governor had all but disappeared from the scene, and Taher had gone and made him a martyr. He had turned an executioner into a victim, a glorious example of civic virtue and self-sacrifice for generations to come, thus perpetuating the eternal fraud.

# OTHER NEW YORK REVIEW CLASSICS*

*   *For a complete list of titles, visit www.nyrb.com or write to:*
    *Catalog Requests, NYRB, 435 Hudson Street, New York, NY 10014*